The River Home

by

Denis Dauphinee

For Nick —
Hope you like the story —
See if you can find the
masterbation scene in it !

Dee Dauphinee

North
Country
Press

The River Home

ISBN 978-0-945980-75-9

Library of Congress Control Number: 2013951721

Theresa Cucinotti Photography – front cover image

Tom Merchant, Rocks & Sticks Photography – back cover image

Dick Charles, drawing of the wet fly

North Country Press
Unity, Maine

For Lisa Darlin

ONE

Ennis surveyed his surroundings while Doc put away his equipment. This was everything a brook in the Maine woods should be. It was spring-fed and clear. The trees were old and close enough to the water's edge so they kept the water temperature cool in the heat of summer. At the tail of the pool, the current cut under the bank from which the lobelia grows and the ferns hang down. Below the ferns there was a sandy spot, and in the sand there were some tracks, probably from a weasel or a small raccoon wandering and sniffing, looking for frogs. The pool was a place where trout could live, and it was perfect.

Doc and Ennis continued on their morning walk.

Winter comes early in northern Maine, and spring comes late, but when spring does finally show, its pastoral beauty is met with excitement by those hardy souls who've survived the snows, and thoughts turn to planting and to fishing. While the western part of Maine's northern most county is a vast, dense expanse of forests and woodlands, the eastern half is the great St John Valley; beautiful meadows, potato fields and clean, tastefully appointed farms and cottages line the highways. The rolling hills resemble the farmland of western Pennsylvania, a landscape in stark contrast to the rugged coastline to the south. As travelers drive north in Maine towards Canada, they are met with a distinct change that's intangible, yet definitely perceptible. The farther north you go, the pace of life gets slower, unless you go during the harvest season, or at planting time, or if it's late fall and every farm is scrambling to prepare for winter. So maybe life isn't slower, but it *seems* slower, and there's something liberating about northern Maine. Those who were raised there understand from a young age there is something special about the place, and those that visit from away (if they have a soul), quickly learn to appreciate the bucolic beauty and attainable wildness.

At the lower end of the North Maine Woods, a large network of rivers and streams drain the densely forested highlands along the border with New Brunswick. They are waters famous for the fish they hold. These woodlands have a fair road traveling east-west from Interstate 95 that crosses several of the more well-known rivers in the area. For some miles the road travels with the West Branch of the Penobscot River, winding upstream past a huddle of small camps, cottages, farmhouses and log cabins, past the two churches and Dr. Arno Warren's Family Practice office, past the tiny elementary school to the town of Roslyn. The road ends at the far side of town – the west side. Beyond the town are only logging roads, skidder trails, tote roads and the narrow, muddy, moose trails that seem to wander incoherently in every direction as if the moose were lost, or had no particular place to go. Inevitably, the paths lead to the river's bank, or to the shore of a pond hidden deep in the woods.

Roslyn is remarkable in northern Maine because of its proximity to the world-class trout and salmon fishing, and because of the many well-known fishing guides and anglers the town has produced for over a century. Every spring, dozens of guides show up in town, either working on their own or for one of the local guide services, or to guide for one of the two fly shops in town. Many of them are college students from Colby, Bowdoin or the University of Maine, but some are middle-aged men who work in the woods during winter. Following close behind the guides are the "sports" that arrive in droves in their SUVs and SAABs. Some are wealthy, some not, and some are in-between. In the middle of this influx of people are the dyed-in-the-wool, full-on fishing bums who can't help but fish...a lot. Roslyn is a *fly fishing* town; in fact, for a mile on either side of town the West Branch is "Fly Fishing Only" water. Fly fishing only or not, it has always been good water. Legend has it the town was named after Roslyn Chapel by an early settler named Buzzle, a lumber speculator and surveyor, who happened to be a serious fly rodder. When he found the valley and stumbled onto the West Branch, he caught salmon and trout by the boatload, and he was sure he had found his Holy Grail.

The town – *Roz* to the locals – sits in a long cove of deadwater in the Penobscot River system where you can travel by boat into Jackson Lake. The cove is so large most tourists think it's a lake and not part of the river. Main Street is set back from the water's edge far enough to be lined on both sides with gift shops, eateries, and boat houses. The edge of town farthest from the water (the *far side* of town), is where the school, the town office, and most of the residences are located.

There are a few good-size buildings in town, erected by long-gone lumber barons. They were built mostly on the water side of Main Street, in the old Federal style, and now hold various offices and studios. Ennis Gray's fly shop, the "Gray's Ghost" occupies the ground floor at No. 12 Main Street.

When visitors look down Main Street in the evening, they often can't help but appreciate the deep, warm feeling of community; of *belonging*. The shops close early. The Gray's Ghost Fly Shop closes at four o'clock in the afternoon, even though it's widely known Ennis would do more business if he stayed open till six o'clock. But the Riverdriver stays open late, and so does the Hungry Hound. The extent of the night-life of Roslyn is the Rexall Drug which stays open until nine o'clock except on Sundays. Not exactly Vegas.

Still, there is almost always some activity near the water, even late at night; the full, sometimes tipsy, native files out of the Riverdriver, stops on the sidewalk to zip up his jacket and gazes up the cove towards the lake, watching the little silver flecks of light shimmer on the tips of the waves, even though he's seen it a thousand times since childhood. Or there's the coughing pedestrian adroitly making his way up the drug store steps. The scene is always there, no matter the season, and the scene can make you feel – *involved* – even communal. And the scene can make you feel the melancholic slippage of time.

******

The sun on this April morning was slanting through the balsam and cedars, peering down the river trail a half-mile from town as it winds down to the Penobscot, all along the way sending little routes down to the water where anglers try every run, rapid, riffle and pool. Dr. Arno Warren and his friend Ennis emerged from the edge of town and walked speedily along the trail. They kept up a quick pace. A stranger might think they were in a hurry. Even though both men were over sixty, the good doctor kept up a running commentary about nearly everything natural—the trees, the weather, the chickadees in the cedar branches, and how the warm weather might bring off an early Quill Gordon hatch.

"A hatch would be great!" said Ennis. "I just got in a big batch of Adams' and Gold-Ribbed Hare's Ears down at the shop from Benny." This was as long a response one would hear from Ennis to one of Doc's dissertations, which was, incidentally, just fine with both parties.

The doctor, in spite of the sunshine, wore a battered waxed cotton packer rain hat from L.L. Bean which looked distinguished with his white hair. His outer garment was a twenty-four-year-old purple Patagonia anorak, a jacket he wore in all four seasons that he had tried many times to throw away but couldn't. Gray, five years younger, made sure to match strides as if he was afraid he would miss something Doc Warren had to say. Ennis's clothing tended toward the non-descript, his customary style. The two had for forty years walked together almost every day, played bridge together almost every Wednesday night, cribbage almost every Sunday, dined together a couple of times a week—and Ennis's wife almost never minded. The doctor had never married. He had built a blissful, comfortable life in the community. Over time, Doc had evolved into a local statesman, philanthropist and philosopher in a town chock full of philosophers; Dickie Hill, for example, who ran the transfer station just outside of town, held a Masters of Arts in French Literature from the University of Michigan. Dickie left town for good after he went to use the two-seater outhouse at the dump, and had locked himself inside before he realized there was a yearling black bear in there already. He couldn't use the outhouse – or any other bathroom for that matter – for two weeks. Dickie got so bound up, he was sitting with his head in his hands in the little booth from where he operated the dumpster compactor. He got up, walked out to the side of the road and stuck his thumb in the air. Someone gave him a ride as far as Millinocket and nobody has seen him for eight years.

"Look," Doc said, without slowing his pace, "look down there." They had come to one of the forks in the path where they could see a part of the river where it made a sharp turn to the east, and then tumbled downhill with roiling class three rapids. It was pretty, but that particular bend pool wasn't one of the best known fishing spots, although it was known to hold brook trout, and at certain times of year, landlocked salmon. A light green speck was visible against the darker green and black water, next to and slightly downstream from one of the large boulders protruding from the surface. "Speak of the devil! Unless I'm wrong, that's our young Benny," the doctor said. "I recognize the rhythm...and the wide loop he throws when nymphing."

(Nymphs are flies fished underwater, and require a slightly different casting technique.)

Ennis asked, "I know we haven't fished that pool together, but have you fished it lately, Arno?"

"Haven't for years...but if Ben Garrison's fishing it, you can bet it's productive."

"Ayuh," replied Ennis, who watched pensively the angler working the pool. "I wonder if he's using the same Hare's Ears he sold me last week?"

Both friends continued up the path, Dr. Warren rattling on about how hackmatack trees don't have a tap root, and can be pushed over with a tractor or even draft horses. He told how their roots were used for making ships' knees to hold up the decks, back when ships were made of wood and had souls. Ennis knew this, of course, but listened happily and looked as interested as he could.

TWO

Twenty-three years earlier, it had been an auspicious start for "the Boys", as they were called by some of the local citizens. The Boys were a small group of men who used each other quite effectively to avoid their own families. While they often told their spouses they were called upon to help a friend in need, in fact, they spent most of their time talking...about current events, their beloved Roslyn, state government, and "the Feds". (None of them, except Doc and Ennis, knew precisely who "the Feds" really were, but that didn't stop "the Boys" from pontificating about them.) It was Doc who often kept the conversations from approaching a high level of unimportance. Mostly, the guys talked about fly fishing, which they all *did* know something about.

Arno Warren had been a child of privilege. His physician father could afford to send him to an expensive prep school in New Hampshire where, while a student, Arno taught Nordic skiing and sailing. It was also where the athletic boy was introduced to the high art of fly fishing by one of the young teachers. The attraction took root, and Arno would be in love with the fly rod for the rest of his life. He worked for a few years in Montana and in South America as a fishing guide before enrolling in medical school.

He was smitten with fly fishing. After a pilgrimage to northern Maine for a fishing trip upon completing his residency, he turned down several job offers in practices in the city, and put up a shingle in Roslyn. It was springtime, and for the first few months in practice the young Dr. Warren became concerned that his decision to start his career in such a rural place was a mistake. He feared his skills would deteriorate over time, and eventually he would become bored professionally. He wasn't quite sure how such a fate would weigh against the "benefit" of living close to world-class fly fishing. The troubles coming through the door were important enough to those who were sick, yet made for a pretty mundane patient load for a new physician. His cases included a dog bite, a broken ankle, a case of chronic fatigue, a dislocated finger, a couple seeking marriage counseling (at least, the wife was), a short run of allergy problems, a fishing fly in the neck, another in an ear, two in scalps, one in an elbow, and another square between the shoulder blades, which took some digging to get out. There was one bad case of poison ivy, and one sick five-year-old who uncovered a big bag of ribbon candy in the bottom of a buffet drawer, and ate the whole thing before being discovered— which probably would have been all right, except the candy was estimated to be twenty-two years old. After one gentleman showed up at the office as a walk-in and (after having his vitals recorded and filling out a complete health history form) basically just wanted to complain about how bad the black flies were that spring, Doc Warren became convinced he had made the wrong decision. Then three things happened to change his mind forever.

Near the end of June, Dr. Warren had found a nice run of riffles just below where Whitney Brook flows quietly into the West Branch. There had been a nice, predictable caddis fly hatch going off sporadically all afternoon, and Doc had caught three fat salmon and a few brookies with a #18 caddis pupa pattern called a Sheff's Special. He worked his way downstream to a rather large bend pool and found a nice rock big enough for him to stand behind. From there, he could wade a bit out of the main current and cast to all of the best feeding lanes along the edges of the main ripples. It being twilight, he worried he might not be able to wade out of the water easily after dark. He lit his pipe, surveyed the water for a while, and then studied the early evening sky. He noticed some large flies cruising upstream, about twelve feet off the water. They were flying deliberately and straight, not fluttering in all directions as some of the earlier caddis flies had been. These were definitely mayflies, and *big* ones. He was about to reach for one of the fly boxes in his vest – the big box with the larger Hendrickson dries in it, trying to match the size of the naturals – when he caught sight of a rise about twenty feet away. He glanced in that direction just in time to see another fish rise and before he could turn his attention back to the fly box there was another...and another! He looked again to the sky. Clouds of mayflies were swarming upstream in a purposeful orgy in flight! Doc deftly swiped his hat above his head and caught one of the big flies for inspection. This was one of the famous Hexagenia hatches he had heard about, and read about in countless angling magazines. He knew that being on the water for an epic nighttime "Hex" hatch was often a major event in the life of a fly fisherman. Doc also knew that in Maine fishermen often mistook Green Drakes for Hexagenias – a completely different insect – but there was no doubt that night; these were definitely Hexagenias, Great Leadwinged Drakes. He tried to stay calm and fumbled quickly through his five fly boxes until he found the one with the big mayfly patterns. There were some #8 Yellow

Hornbergs, but he never had much faith in them, and some spinners of the same size. There were a few old, sparsely tied #6 Wulffs, and a few #8 Green Drakes. They would have to do. Fish were rising everywhere now, some as close as six feet from where he stood. With dusk deepening as he pulled the Wulff from the box, he accidentally knocked loose the Drake fly, which fell into the water at his feet. He watched it float away for two seconds before there was a silver flash in the darkness. A salmon! Not three feet away, the fish took the fly under the water! Whether the landlocked ate it or spit it, Arno didn't know. Now there were only two Drakes left. He tried to stay calm and carefully tied the Wulff artificial to his tippet. He made sure to tie a good knot, and applied a little floatant to the body of the fly. As he stripped out some line for his first cast, he started to survey the pool for the biggest rise, when he spotted the "one" at the tail of the pool. He was shocked to see another man directly opposite him, standing in a casting position, watching him. He hadn't seen him—the stranger had apparently been at the pool first. The angler had a fish on. Arno watched the man play the salmon calmly and quickly, and released it straight from the landing net. Doc worried that he might be intruding but the hatch wouldn't last all night. In the waning light it would be hard to make his way to a new spot in time. He got the angler's attention. "Am I all right here?"

"You betcha! Wet your line!" was the reply.

Doc flicked his rod tip to let out the slack line. After two false casts, made a nice cast and the fly landed about ten feet above the spot where he had seen the largest rises. Then he made two quick upstream mends. Doc couldn't help but notice that his fellow angler had another fish on. Arno watched intently as his big fly drifted perfectly past the spot he was targeting. Still, Doc wasn't ready for the strike. The salmon swirled to the fly so fast, he missed the hookset and the fish was gone. He hauled the line hard with his left hand, raised the rod tip and waited calmly while the line unfurled behind him, then casted forward with a slight left-hand hook at the end. There was no need for any mend of the fly line. As soon as the fly touched the water, the fish broke the surface. It didn't look especially large in the dark, but as the rod strained and the fish ran, it felt heavy indeed.

As Arno kept pressure on his fish, he felt a faint lull in the strain on the rod tip. Suddenly there was surge, and an explosion of water not thirty feet away, as the salmon leapt from the depths. The silver body looked unreal for a moment in the June moonlight, like the whole scene was a painting and Arno was in it, part of it. The salmon was iridescent silver with the tiniest flecks of lavender picked up by the soft light. The fish shook its head twice, then slapped back into the water on its side.

While the salmon was still suspended in the air, the angler downstream yelled through a cupped hand, "Bow to her!" – a reference to the old-timer's notion that one lowers the rod tip slightly when the fish jumps. "Keep her head up!" Doc's new companion yelled again, "I'll come with my net." Doc did just that...applied gentle pressure on the light, 5X tippet. He tried to move the fish slightly downstream to an eddy which he *hoped* wouldn't be too deep to wade, so he could land this fish. By now it had become clear; this was a very big fish.

Arno did everything he could think of to move the fish around but it had become clear that simple pressure wouldn't move her (or him), upstream or down. He tried to keep his eyes on the line and the water. In his peripheral vision, he could see the stranger wading into the slack water of the eddy, twenty feet away. At this point in the fight, Arno actually started to *think*. He knew this fish was large, but how large? He knew that this water was one of the only rivers left in the country where the average fly fisher had the potential to catch really large salmon – up to eight pounds, in fast-moving water. He knew also he was stuck. He tried coaxing the monster fish by moving the rod pressure first right, then left, but the fish would have none of it. She was holding out on the edge of one of the feeding lanes...just lying there. Doc pictured her there, gills opening as wide as possible, the smashed Wulff hanging out of the corner of her mouth. She was just slightly too far below the stranger, who had been quiet for some time now, his net at the ready. Doc knew if he "yarded" too hard with the rod, it would surely break the tiny tippet. It was at that moment he remembered a tactic his father had taught him while fishing for steelhead in upstate New York. He raised the rod tip slowly, payed out a few feet of line and then executed a beautiful roll cast downstream, between the holding fish and the stranger. Seconds later, with the rod tip held down parallel to the water's surface, he pulled upstream. The slack line in the water's current changed the pressure the fish felt in her mouth to *downstream*. That subtle difference in sensation made her change her position and she tried moving up the river. Arno quickly stripped in line several times before she caught her breath. He was moving her, slowly, into the eddy. At last, she was above the stranger. She was tired now. Arno could guide her easily. When the fish was about five feet above the stranger, the man must have gotten his first good look at her. He peered into the dark water, bent closer for an instant, and then stood straight upright and tossed his net on the river bank. He never took his eyes off the fish. Not two seconds went by before the fellow reached into the water, first with his right arm, then with his left. Out came the fish, her tail firmly in the stranger's right hand, her belly cradled by his left. It became obvious why the net was useless. In an instant, Arno stood next to the man and his fish.

The other fellow held her now just in the water's surface film so she could breath. He started to hand the beast to Arno when Doc said, "No, no...you hold her please." It was no longer Arno's fish...it was *their* fish. Arno held his rod alongside the salmon and inspected the markings he had put near the handle of the rod with nail polish: six inches, then nine, then fourteen and then the last marking was twenty-two inches from the handle. The salmon's tail was well past the last marking. For a moment, Arno thought about keeping the fish. He thought how great it would look mounted above the reception desk at his office, sporting a new, pristine Wulff of the exact same dressing as the one in her mouth now. How Mrs. O'Leary, his receptionist, would get tired of fielding questions about it from every new patient. But he couldn't do it. Arno was not above keeping a fish now and then to eat, but ninety-nine percent of the time he released the fish he caught, to fight another day. This extraordinary fish was clearly over seven pounds, caught on a four-pound tippet.

Arno looked at the stranger now, who had been quietly resuscitating the fish while waiting to see what the owners' intentions were.

"What do you think?" asked Doc.

"Damn," said the stranger, "It's the biggest fish I've ever seen come out of here...actually, it's the biggest fish I've seen come out of anywhere – including Pelletier's (the local grocery store)."

"No," said Arno, "what do you *think?*"

"Well," the stranger said again, "I think it's time she goes home." Doc grinned a little and pulled the barbless fly from the fish's mouth. The stranger gently let go of the fish, its head pointing into the current. Its tail flexed twice, unhurried, and it was gone, into the black water. Arno and the stranger stepped to the bank where Doc, tired himself, plopped onto a rock. "Thanks for everything," Doc said.

"You kidding?" asked the stranger. "That was great." He thrust his hand towards Doc. "Ennis Gray," he said.

"Arno Warren," Doc said, shaking his hand.

"*Doctor* Warren," Ennis acknowledged.

"Yes sir," said Doc, "but please, call me Arno."

"I've been meaning to make an appointment with you..." Ennis said, as they made their way back up the dark trail.

The moon had slipped behind some clouds and it was pitch black by the time Ennis and Doc Warren made their way back to the road. Only a few disoriented Hexagenia remained, flying by in the filtered moonlight, having struck out for the night, only to die a virgin. (This is a big deal to them, as they *get* only one shot at sex...ever.) Doc had a thermos of coffee which they shared in his truck while they talked about "The Fish", and what had just happened on the river. Then, they talked about the Hex hatch. Doc went off on a tangent about his old cane rod, and how lots of people say the bamboo is too heavy and can fatigue a fisherman in the course of a day of fishing. Doc said, "If you're doing it right, you *should* be tired at the end of the day." He continued that cane rods had a different feel to them than all the other rod-building materials and that the grass rods made the angler feel more "connected" to the river, the trees, the fish...to everything around them while they fished (whether they understood it or not). Besides, the newer cane rods weren't much heavier than graphite anyway. Ennis nodded and sighed; he just didn't have the market for the bamboo rods in Roslyn.

"I've been in your shop," Doc said to Ennis. "It's real nice...inviting." He added, "I like the old wood stove you have in the back."

"Thanks. I took that out of the old one-room schoolhouse before they tore it down. It was right next door to your clinic."

"Was it?" asked Doc.

"Yup. Before Roz was a flyfishing town. (In Roslyn, flyfishing is said and spelled as one word.) It was an end-of-the-line depot town for the railroad," Ennis explained. "A hundred years ago, there were more people living here than there is now. Twice as many kids crammed into that school. Now, with the lumberin' operations gone, we can fit 'em all in one room again." There was a pause, and Ennis shook his head, "Can't get over that fish." Then he asked Doc, "Did you happen to notice the stuffed salmon over the counter?"

"Of course," replied the doctor.

"Well, your fish was a lot bigger than that," said Ennis.

"If that's so, we should name it," replied Doc.

Ennis half-closed one eye. "I had a passel of aunts," he said. "There was this one, Matilda, who was bigger than all the rest."

"Perfect," Doc proclaimed.

"Well, Doc, I'd better get home or my wife will think I drowned in the Big Eddy, and she'll have started her list of what to sell off first."

Doc held out his hand again and said, "It was my pleasure." They shook again.

"See you soon, Doc!" said Ennis as he jumped into his truck.

The friendship that developed that night would prove to be a long lasting one. Its energy would positively affect the entire community. Ennis and Arno would be inexorably connected for the rest of their lives.

THREE

As Doc Warren's first summer rolled along, his patient load remained the same...slow and mundane. He liked the fact that he was able to give a great deal of attention to each patient – much more than he could have in any practice in Boston. It wasn't long before he realized he was building relationships in Roslyn unlike any he had previously known. He also became rather proud of his office. He liked its simple furniture, the rustic look of the waiting room, and the carefully chosen reading material. He subscribed to magazines and papers meant to inspire, not just to occupy the minds of the people. The lack of a television was a conscious decision. Doc was also very fond of the so-called "Wall of Shame," a bulletin board screwed to the back of the door of one of the exam rooms. Whenever someone came in with a fly stuck in some part of their anatomy, Doc would always give the victim two options: surrender the fly to the Wall of Shame, or be charged for an office visit. By the end of August, the bulletin board was appointed with thirty-three flies. Every week, he would pluck one or two flies from the wall and study the materials in each lure. Doc learned to tie a lot of local fly patterns that first summer.

Ennis Gray eventually came in to the office to try different creams and ointments for the eczema on his hands. On each visit, the two friends spoke affectionately about their fish, now known by all as Matilda, and invariably one of the two men would say, "That was salmon-chanted evening!" They both would chuckle, and they never tired of it.

Gray's Ghost Fly Shop was downtown between Pelletier's Grocery and St. Mary's church. Doc became one of the regulars there (the fly shop, not the church). For many winters he would frequent the shop to drink coffee, smoke his pipe, tie flies and tell fish stories. Often, he could perform all four tasks simultaneously. Doc and Ennis would sit on the couch or in one of the rocking chairs in the back of the shop. The sitting area looked over the wooden displays filled with flies and the racks with pegs on them that held leaders, tippets, clippers and strike indicators. The two men would entertain each other and the rest of the boys who frequented the little shop. It was a latter-day Man Cave. Also in the back, there was a small wood stove and a little square table for card playing, or map reading, or pinochle games. Midwinter weekends were spent tying flies with the wood stove blasting heat, or pouring over a tattered old DeLorme gazetteer, looking for new places to fish the next spring. Thirty years later, the winter days are still the same.

At least for Doc, the relationships were the thing. While small town life has its appeal to many people, there are some drawbacks. For one, the schools become quite provincial. The teachers are often very good (and are good folks), but in the times before the internet they lived in a world with limited outside ideas and thought. Education ran the risk of falling into a bit of a rut. Another problem is a potential lack of culture, and the third is that medical facilities are not always available. As Doctor Warren became more entrenched in the community – and developed more relationships – he took it personally. He could help with the education in town, expand upon its culture (or at least he hoped he could) and beyond his clinic, the nearest medical help would be the hospital thirty miles away in Millinocket, and the closest level-1 trauma center was downstate in Bangor.

The third thing that happened to Doc that first year was the introduction of Benjamin Garrison. Arno arrived at his office on the morning of the first day of July knowing he had only four patients booked in the morning. (With any luck, he would be able to meet Ennis in the afternoon, to try out some new stonefly nymphs he'd recently tied. These flies were a new pattern of Little Yellow Stonefly that Doc recently pulled from the skin of a visiting angler from New Hampshire. The fellow looked like a hardcore, old school, "flyfishing only" river bum who said he was sleeping in his car for the week. The patient showed up to the office, still in his patched waders and never took them off. So, Doc thought his fly might be worth a try. Arno tied a few right there in his office before retiring the original to the Wall of Shame.) When Doc entered the waiting room, he noticed a very attractive young mother, perhaps twenty years old, with a boy about four years old.

Doc greeted his receptionist, Mrs. O'Leary. He smiled at the young mother as he passed and gave a quick wink to the little boy, sitting perfectly still in his straight-backed chair. The doctor couldn't help but notice the light grey color of the boy's eyes, offset by his sandy brown hair. He had a sad, interested look in the eyes. He also noticed the boy was sitting crooked in the chair, but wasn't slouching, and had an asymmetric torso. Doc noticed the child's affect— his bearing, his sad yet attentive gaze. And in that slight moment in time, the doctor felt something for the boy. He wasn't sure what it was, but he felt *something.*

Doc always read the New Patient Chart before seeing each person. The boy's chart read; "Benjamin Garrison: **Date of birth**: July 1, 1985 **age**: 4 **Weight**: 31 lbs. **Mother**: Lisa Garrison **Father**: Wesley Garrison (deceased) **Complaint**: Problem with bones."

When Dr. Warren entered the exam room he shook hands with Mrs. Garrison, and then with Benjamin. Mrs. O'Leary had dressed the boy in a johnnie and he held a *National Geographic* in his lap. Doc looked at the boy, smiled, tapped a spot on the chart and said, "Happy birthday, Benjamin."

Ben didn't smile, but looked at the doctor shyly and said in a soft, meek voice, "Thank you."

"So, we're having problems with some bones, are we?" asked Doc. Benjamin only nodded. Doc looked to Mrs. Garrison.

"Yes, Doctor," she said. "When Benny was born, I took him to the Medical Center in Bangor because his left arm didn't work too well, and his back (she pointed to the back of his neck) was crooked. The doctors down there told me I had to tie his left arm to the crib at night, to keep it elevated." She went on. "They said his shoulder blade stayed in the wrong place when he was still a fetus. There are some things he can't do well, but he's coping with it like a trooper. I just wanted to know if there's something else we should be doing."

"Well, let's take a look, would that be all right?" asked Doc. He asked Benjamin to stand facing a wall. Doc could see clearly enough the boy's neck was a little short, and that he stood listing to one side. "Can you stand up straighter?" he asked. Ben did, with some effort. "Does it hurt to stand straight?"

"No, sir," Ben said softly. The doctor opened the boy's johnnie enough to look at his back. Ben's left scapula was clearly malpositioned – it was riding higher than the right one, and appeared smaller.

"Would you bend over as far as you can, Ben, and let your arms dangle?" asked Doc. Ben did, and the doctor ran both hands along the boy's spine. When he did, Ben jumped almost imperceptibly. "Hands cold?" asked Doc.

"Little bit," replied Ben.

"Yes, Mrs. O'Leary likes the AC up high." By now, Doc's hand was feeling the boy's neck, and had felt the borders of both scapulae. He noted the right felt normal, but the left one was in fact, higher and rotated a bit out of place.

Doc Warren had Benjamin bend, twist and turn. He asked him to walk on his toes, then his heels. He had him stand on each leg, one at a time, and to jump up and down. Doc measured the boy's leg lengths and checked the tightness of his hamstrings. He had Ben sit on the side of the exam table and checked every reflex possible. Doc then tested sensation on both of the boy's legs, both arms, his neck, torso, face, feet, and hands. It was quite a workout for both of them. All the while Doc would make quick notes on his clipboard; sometimes he'd write something; other times he would make a check, or a little line. "Would you mind lying down for me?" asked the doctor.

The doctor felt, and gently pushed on Ben's abdomen – first near his ribs, then over his kidneys, and then the lower belly. He checked his pulse and respirations, and then listened with his stethoscope to the young patient's heart and lungs. Mrs. Garrison remained silent during the entire exam, and so did Ben, unless he was asked a question. Doc couldn't help but notice again a gentle, intelligent quality about Ben, and in such a young boy. "Next, I'd like to get an X-ray." Doc asked Mrs. Garrison. "We usually try not to x-ray children, but I'd like to get a couple of views to keep as a baseline." She nodded approval with a slight smile. Doc then asked Benjamin if he minded getting his picture taken with a special camera. He also nodded and tried to smile.

Once the X-rays were developed, Doc Warren went back to the exam room where the Garrisons waited. He smiled and asked Ben's mother, "Would you mind if Benjamin sat with Mrs. O'Leary for a bit while we talked?"

"Oh, no...that would be fine. We've known Ethel all our lives," she said. They took Benjamin out to the waiting room where Mrs. O'Leary was waiting.

"I've got out some games and blocks for you to play with, Benny" she said.

"Thanks, Ethel, that's sweet," Mrs. Garrison said, "but Benny will probably just want something to read." The young boy immediately took his original seat, and picked up a magazine. Ben's mom bent down to speak, "I'll be with Dr. Warren for a few minutes, honey, and then we'll go for a walk down by the river." The boy smiled approvingly.

Doc led the young mother back to his office and they sat down opposite each other. While Doc was always very professional, he was still struck by Lisa Garrison's beauty; her fine, brown hair, her high cheek bones and most of all, her bright green, intelligent and somewhat sad eyes.

"Mrs. Garrison, Benjamin has several things going on," he started. She stiffened in her chair a little. Doc smiled and lifted the fingers of one hand slightly, palm toward her, "Nothing threatening," he said. "It's obvious he has some skeletal issues," Doc went on.

"Ben has what's called Sprengle's Deformity, and along with that, he has some scoliosis." The young woman nodded, seriously. Doc told her Sprengle's on its own isn't something that would deny someone a good quality of life – a normal life. However, the deformity is often associated with other problems, including scoliosis. "There is another, more serious syndrome sometimes present, but I've ruled it out with the X-rays," Doc said. He went on, "I'm going to make some copies of the films and send them down to a friend in Boston to confirm that. So, let's talk about what this means," he said. "His shoulder blade will always be the way it is, but it could change position some when he goes through puberty, and over time he'll compensate for it. I don't foresee any serious problems with it. The more active he is the better. The scoliosis is another matter," said Doc. "It's not too bad at this point, but we'll have to watch him." Lisa lowered her head a little. "Every three months I'd like to see him and evaluate things," Doc said. "If the curvature gets worse, we may have to fit him for a brace. When he gets a little older, I'll give you some exercises for Ben to do."

Mrs. Garrison was attentive and smiled and said, "OK, we will."

Doc Warren said, "This is an orthopaedic problem, Mrs. Garrison, and he should be evaluated by an orthopaedic surgeon. If you'd like, I could make an appointment for you with an orthopaedist in Bangor."

Mrs. Garrison was quick to say, "Oh no, I think we'll go with your plan...it sounds good to me." She looked at her lap again. "You don't know Ben very well," she said. "He does have some problems with his bones...but he's exceptional in so many ways. Everybody knows that." She went on, "He's only four, but he reads chapter books. He's real good with his hands, and he can tie flies already." Mrs. Garrison paused for a second. "You see, Doc, he's getting to the age when the other kids will call him names, like "no neck" or something like that." She said, "I just want the best for Benny, Doctor."

Doc waited, and then said to Mrs. Garrison, "I can see Benny is a great kid. You should be nothing but proud. I also don't want you to be worried about the cost of office visits every three months. You can pay whatever you can, and work it out with Mrs. O'Leary. I do need a consult from an orthopaedist, though." Doc thought for a moment, then said, "I know a new orthopod in Bangor who's obsessed with fly fishing." Lisa smiled. "Maybe if I invite him up here for a little fishing, I know he'll go over Benjamin's X-rays...won't cost a cent," Doc said with a smile. Lisa Garrison tried unsuccessfully to hold back a tear. She knew that she had found a kind man in Doctor Warren, and a good spirit. As they left the office to collect Benjamin in the waiting room, Doc turned to Mrs. Garrison and said, "Maybe Benjamin could tie a hometown fly for my friend when he comes – for reading the X-rays."

Lisa smiled again, "I'm sure he'd like to."

Ben was sitting perfectly still in the exact same position, thumbing through his third *National Geographic*, looking at a photo of Machu Picchu.

"Let's go, honey," said Mrs. Garrison. "Say thank you to the Doctor." Ben stood up, neatened the stack of magazines, being careful not to put a wrinkle in any of the covers, and then turned to Doc and shook his hand.

"Thank you," he said quietly.

"You are most welcome, son," replied Doc.

"Thank you, Ethel," said Lisa, "I'll call for the next appointment." As the two Garrisons walked to the door, Benjamin looked up at his mother and said, "Mommy...what's an Inca?"

The friendships, Matilda, the clear need for the medical clinic, his desire to help Benny— Doc Warren knew he was in Roslyn to stay. Within a few years Doc had dug himself into the fabric of the community. And stay he did, for these twenty-three years. He even told the Boys one night after drinking Cognac he wanted to be "buried in town when I go under, not down in Mass." They all drank to that.

FOUR

Ennis and Doc, at the start of one of their walks, had come to the edge of town to the Nielson farmstead, one of the few working farms in a village once known for timber harvesting. In the dooryard of the farm stood a tall, thin man in his sixties (he was near to the same age as the Boys, but looked fifteen years older). He stood bowed over his '49 Ford 8N tractor, with heat rising in a vapor from the engine shroud as if the old thing was breathing hard from having just plowed a half-acre side field. The warm reek of freshly turned topsoil hung pleasantly in the air.

"Wonderful smell," said Doc Warren to Ennis, "so rich." He waved a greeting to the farmer. "Always hard at work, eh, John?"

"Ayuh. The work never stops for a famah this close to the woods." The farmer nodded at the tractor. "The plow hates them rocks." John stared at the Boys with his pale blue eyes and smiled. "How's the sawbones business, Doc?"

"Nice and slow," replied Arno.

"How's the fishin', Ennis?" John asked.

"Only been twice, but the guides are all in, and they're booked, so life is good."

John said, "Saw some of them mayflies you showed me down by the brook yestiday."

Ennis smiled and nodded his head.

"How's our lovely Annie?" piped in the Doctor, his slightly upper-crust Boston accent contrasting sharply with the farmer's thick Mainer speech.

"Just fine, Doc," replied John, "She's hahd at it with the second plantin' of cohn up in the top field. Crows got most o' the first plantin', but I shot one and tied it to a stick in the field...they won't come back till a coyote hauls it off. She's a workah, that girl. Wheah you boys headin' off to today?" asked John.

Ennis fielded this question before Doc could chime in, just to keep things fresh. "Up Lewis Brook to the old trestle to have lunch and beat the bushes to find out what's hatching."

The farmer looked incredulous. "Why aren't you fellers takin' fishin' rods?"

Doc answered, "Well, John, sometimes it's good to look at fishing from another angle. To be a great angler one must learn as much as one can about all aspects of catching fish – what they eat and when they eat it, study what their vision capabilities are, you know...their biology. Do it enough and it can become as interesting or as fun as actually catching fish."

Before Doc was done philosophizing, Ennis noticed he had lost John. For a man who worked ninety hours a week just to keep a farm going, it was too much to think about, chasing so hard after a hobby. Besides, John was still sore that he could no longer dunk a worm in the river where he had as a child, now that the state had ruled it *Fly Fishing Only*. John was staring blankly at Doc until the old physician finally spoke. "Well then, good day to you, John!"

"Good luck with them bugs!" said the farmer, as he turned back to the tractor.

"Mahogany Duns," mumbled Ennis as they left.

"Say again?" asked Doc.

"Oh, what John saw for mayflies...must have been Mahoganies this early."

"Right," Doc nodded.

They strode off up the dirt road towards the bridge that Lewis Brook babbled under, and they soon saw Annie Nielson planting one of the rows where the contour of the field dipped close to the roadside. She was bent over ninety degrees and was tearing small holes in the row of black plastic mulch, her feet wide apart straddling the plastic. She would rise up and pull two or three seeds from a canvas painter's pouch tied around her waist. She would bend over again and drop the seeds into the hole and then brush a little soil to cover them. She took a big step and repeated the process over and over again. Her pretty, lustrous blond hair fell below her shoulders, lifting in the breeze as she worked. On her feet were calf-high Muck boots, and above her athletic, shapely legs she wore a cotton skirt, which also played in the wind. Doing field work in a skirt...that was just Annie's way. She was singing "Sweet Baby James" to herself, a little off key. The Boys stopped on the shoulder of the road.

"Hello, Annie!" Doc Warren hailed her. She rose up and immediately ran toward the old friends, her eyes smiling as always.

"How are my favorite men?" she asked.

"Well, we're surviving, which is good," Ennis answered.

"We've got two sports coming to stay with us! Today!" Annie exclaimed.

"Here at the farm?" Doc was curious. "I thought your father was sort of...against fly fishermen in principle."

She laughed. "Since we lost so many crops last year because of the wet spring, he says if he can't fish the river any longer, he might as well hook some tourists. I love the idea. We're going to take in boarders whenever the campground is full. I think it's going to be great. They both are students at Dartmouth. I'll have someone other than Dad to talk to at mealtime. Oh, and Ennis, Dad put up a bulletin board with local info like where to eat, a map of the river pools and such and he put on it your contact info along with a map to your shop."

"This is all quite a new development for you," replied Ennis. "Please thank your father for me."

"I will, if I ever finish this planting!" she called back to the Boys as she skipped back to the plastic row. "Hope you find something interesting to observe, Arno!"

Annie at times called the elders by their first name. It was just part of her flirtatious, engaging manner. The Boys put themselves to the narrowing trail.

"She's pretty amazing, Arno," Ennis observed. "She could be a model in any city, with her beauty and grace, and she's smart enough to pursue any education, yet she chooses to stay here...on the farm." Ennis said, "She represents the best of her generation...at least around here."

"Yes," Doc agreed, "but there are others around." There were some things Doc couldn't say about Annie, to anyone. She had been a regular patient of Doc's for all of her life, and since her mother had died when she was just fifteen, she had over the years confided in Doc Warren in a great many things beyond the normal health issues and vaccinations. Along with Mrs. O'Leary and an aunt who lived downriver in East Millinocket, Doc had helped her through much of the wonder, angst and curiosity that's involved with becoming a woman. While Doc always recommended she involve her father in even the most delicate issues, John was rarely consulted. She knew her dad better than anyone.

Although she was at the top of her class in high school, she chose not to accept any of the offers of scholarships. Her father needed her at home. John tried to convince her to go to college regardless, but a loving duty to an aging father won out. One of the confidences related to Doc throughout the years, was her secret desire—her craving, really— of a more educated, grander life. The doctor had to remain quiet and keep these matters to himself.

****

When the Boys reached the bridge over Lewis Brook, they never broke stride, and after straddling the wooden guard rail, hiked deliberately up the right side of the stream, hopping from boulder to boulder along the water's edge. The woods were not too thick, as they hadn't been cut in over one hundred years. It was a beautiful brook. There were a few hardwood trees scattered here and there, but it ran mostly through a cedar forest – trees spaced nicely with great mats of thick, green moss to walk on. Up from the moss grew tall ferns close to the water's edge, ferns that in a couple of months would serve as landing pads for iridescent blue and green damsel flies. Every few yards were large granite boulders, smoothed by the glaciers, perfect for sitting on to rest the weary.

About a quarter-mile upstream, there is a section where the terrain gets steep and there is a series of six little plunge pools tumbling down through the cedars and above those are two long, deep pools with mossy, overhanging banks on both sides. A little farther, the current slows and the trees open up into a big meadow with ancient, dead cedars, tall grass, and freshly sprouted Indian Pitcher plants are everywhere underfoot. There the stream wanders lazily in the open sunlight. That is where the "deadwater" is.

The men stopped alongside the last pool before the slow deadwater. They found a couple of flat-topped boulders, and had a lunch of sliced summer sausage and extra-sharp cheddar cheese. (Doc was fond of saying cheddar cheese should be so sharp it bites back.) They drank some coffee from the same thermos they shared on the night they met twenty-three years earlier, making some vague, tentative plans to fish some of the rivers and streams over in the Rangely area in the coming months.

When the conversation dried up, Doc rummaged around in his day pack and found his seine. Most times when he fished, Doc liked to carry the small piece of fine mesh cloth tied with two dowels that he used to dredge up insects from the stream bottoms. He waded into the water in bare feet to his shins at the foot of the pool, and facing upstream he held the net between his feet. Ennis waded in farther upstream at the head of the pool, turning over football size rocks from the streambed. Doc waited less than a minute, till his feet went numb from the cold, then he closed the two dowels together and came ashore.

Spreading the net open on a flat rock, Doc inspected the half-dozen bugs caught in the cloth. Some squirmed around, while some of them just clung to the net. From his pack he retrieved a small journal with a pen inside, held closed by a rubber band. Next, he pulled a monocular from the breast pocket of his fly vest. After closer inspection, Doc made two entries in his journal:

April 21

> Clingers (x4) short, thick legs- prob. #18...prob. Epeorus P.- Quill Gordons
> Crawlers (x3) prob. Ephemerella.-Hendricksons
> Some long thin nymphs; (x3) black wing pads- look like BWO's
> Case builders (x2) (x5) w/sticks & gravel- Limnephilidae for certain

Lewis Brook in April

> Drys: Adams, Q. Gordons, Hendrx., Blue Winged Olive
> Hair's Ear, Chopped deer-hair caddis, maybe small Maple Syrup.
> Wet: Pheasant tail w/ dark wing case. Hend. Nymph- brown w/gold ribbed

Doc Warren was the only guy in the local fly fishing community to use the Greek and Latin names of the insect's family, order, or genus. Some of the straight-ahead, full-on fly fishing nuts *did* know the fancy names—they just chose not to use them. Whenever a sport came to town throwing words like "Perlodidae" around, the natives would roll their eyes and the offending party could consider himself judged, if he was paying attention. The visitor might be considered by all to be a nice guy, maybe, but bordering on being a tenderfoot, no matter how capable he might be. Worse yet, if God forbid he goes out in a canoe alone and paddles the boat backwards, from the bow seat, or kneels on the floor like you see in some outdoor catalogs, that could label him downright effete. (In Maine, when alone, one paddles a canoe normally from the stern, with rocks or some other weight placed in the bow.)

Doc alone got a pass from the locals on his choice of nomenclature, partly because as a physician he was a scientist, but mostly because he was well loved, respected and accepted in the community.

As Doc made his notes, Ennis sloshed up to him and handed him three more case-building caddis larvae. Doc corrected the count. These are the kinds of things Doc Warren did for fun. Ennis enjoyed it too, but really went along with Doc for the camaraderie, the exercise, and edification. If Doc wasn't his friend, it is doubtful Ennis would've taken the time to conduct this sort of nerdy research expedition. Ennis did however regularly use the information from his trips with Doc to outfit his guides at the fly shop with proper flies. Doc never suspected that Ennis wasn't simply enthralled by the learning process, with him as a teacher.

Ennis looked over the pool again while Doc put away his equipment. This was the brook of spring-fed water. This was the brook with shade trees, the ferns, and the tracks in the sand. It *was* perfect. Ennis didn't mention the tracks in the sand to Doc, because it was late in the afternoon and he wanted to get going. The Boys, while on their walks, did discuss just about everything of importance, but Ennis would often keep some observations to himself in an effort to keep sane.

****

Annie, her planting done, ran to the house to make sure everything was ready for the two new guests, the farm's first guests. Typical of Maine farmhouses, the parlor is called the living room and it was medium size and well furnished. On either side of a large picture window were two big overstuffed chairs. The adjacent dining room contained an antique table with a lace table cloth. On the walls were photographs of Annie's parents when they were young, their wedding picture, and a collection of old images of men and horses working in the woods. The kitchen was bigger. It had a large wood-burning cook stove astride the white and gray linoleum floor, newly washed by Annie, which shone in the afternoon sunlight. There was a large, rustic table that could seat as many as eight in the middle of the room, large enough for the family John and Adelis Nielson had hoped for.

She puffed up the pillows in the already plush chairs, checked the flower arrangements in the vases on both tables, and inspected the floor one more time for field dirt. Then she stared out the window and down the driveway. For a moment she daydreamed, filled with excitement. People were actually coming to the farm, she thought to herself, someone from away, with new stories, new experiences, new ideas—*someone* new.

In her lonely childhood Annie had lived a life of daydreams. She dreamed of life off the farm. She loved the old place, surely, but she felt the ancient inevitable desire for love, admiration, romance and excitement. As a teenager, she would lie in the top field on sunny spring days and dream an impossible dream wherein she saw herself married to someone wealthy, someone who would take her to see the world. Annie longed to travel and to learn. She wanted to experience life in the fullest and always try new things, new foods, new *anything.* Anything but the same drudgery of subsistence farming. She knew she was smart enough, she was valedictorian in her class and scored high enough on her SAT's to get into almost any university. She had been told that she was the prettiest woman in the county. She knew that she had *some* beauty to offer someone. She also knew she didn't really need a man to travel; she was capable of anything on her own. Yet her love for her father, who had to raise her alone during some of the most difficult years, had bound her to the life she now led. Her father was incapable of working the farm alone. No one could.

She was still looking out the window when she realized the time. They would be here any moment.

FIVE

"Tom!" yelled the young man in the Jeep Wrangler as the road into town drew nearer. "The West Branch! We'll be in Roslyn in about thirty minutes. Get ready for Nirvana, my friend!" Tom was awake now, at the tail end of the marathon drive from Dartmouth. Chris's voice softened, "I love this town, Tom, this whole place. I swear...I could live here."

"Then you should," replied Tom. "You could manage your stocks from home, and I could come and fish every spring and have a place to stay. I think it's a great idea," Chris just smiled sarcastically and kept driving. Chris was intent on converting Tom to the magic of Roslyn, and the West Branch, and the Machias, and Baxter State Park, and the dozens of great trout and salmon streams in the area. Chris's religion was an honest, free-spirited life, and the rivers were his church – and Roslyn, true to its name, was his chapel. Chris spoke over the hum of the tires on the road, "Like I said, I've never stayed at this farm before so I don't know what to expect. All the rooms at the motel were taken. But it'll be dry and warm, and we won't have to camp—more time on the river."

"Streamers, you think?" asked Tom.

"Oh, we should get a couple of hatches; a caddis hatch around 10:00 or 11:00 in the morning, then some Olives and maybe some Quill Gordons late in the day." The more Chris talked about hatches, the faster the jeep went.

When they drove into Roslyn it was afternoon. Chris wheeled the Jeep past the camps, past the two churches and into Doc Warren's clinic. As he turned in, a new building caught his eye across the street. The two walked into Doc's office to say hello. Doc heard them come in.

"Well," said Doc to Chris, his hand outstretched, "can't stay away from the Great White North?"

Chris shook his hand. "You know I love it! Just wanted to say hi, and to introduce you to Tom Monroe. Tom, this is the famous Doctor Arno Warren."

Doc shook Tom's hand. "And it's not easy being famous, this far in the woods," Doc said with a wink. They all laughed.

"Are you staying at the campground? I might stop by later for a cocktail."

"Actually, no, we're billeting with Mr. Nielson at the farm. When Paul at the campground told us it was full, he said the Nielsons were renting rooms."

"Yes indeed," said Doc, "Ennis and I saw John and Annie this morning on our walk. Annie's quite excited...someone to talk to, I suppose. Not sure about John, though."

"He won't have to entertain us," replied Chris, "we'll take our meals in town and probably will turn in early."

"Annie might want to feed you," said Doc. "She likes to experiment with her cooking, and John's a meat-and-potato guy. She'll like the company—it's just her and her father out there. Have you met Annie?" asked Doc.

"No, why?" said Chris.

Doc shook his head, glanced at both men and said, "Well, if there is a "ten" out there in the universe, Annie is an eleven." Chris cocked his head slightly and looked at Doc a little dubiously; it was strange to hear the older physician say something so...juvenile.

"What is that new building going up across the street?" asked Chris.

"*That* cabin, my friend, is an enigma. Ben Garrison has been working on it all winter. He bought the land from the town for a song, got Graham Toole to yard up eighty peeled logs last fall, and started putting up the walls. He's a hell of a clever guy, and builds beautiful cabins. He's notching all the logs by hand, the old-fashioned way, and places the logs using purlins and a block and tackle."

"What's the enigma?" asked Chris.

"Nobody can figure out why Ben wants to build a new home right in town when he's already built the most attractive, pleasing and tasteful log cabin right on the river, up near where Mattagamon Stream comes in. He seems to be happy out there, and everybody knows it's the nicest place around. Ben's not saying anything about the new place. Not that Ben would talk about it anyway."

"Huh," was all Chris could say as he looked out the window at the pretty, light yellow, perfectly straight log walls with no roof.

The Nielson farmhouse looked like most Aroostook county farms when Chris and Tom arrived at the dooryard. A long, straight gravel drive went up to the barnyard, made a half-circle and turned back to the road. Jutting from the back of the house was an ell that attached to the barn. They drove in, stopped the Jeep, and heaved themselves from the vehicle. John emerged from the barn. "You must be the fishah men," he said.

Chris agreed. "Yes, we are, sir...Chris Phelps." John tried to wipe off the dirt from his hand before shaking, but Chris grabbed it before he could. Nielson liked that.

"Glad ya made it, fellers. It's the first time we've had boardahs, but them's the times we live in. Annie will take good cayah of you, and she's quite the cook. And if you catch some fish along the way, I guess that's all that mattahs."

"Sounds good, Mr. Nielson. This is Tom Monroe."

"Hello, son," said John. "You go to Dahtmuth, too?"

"Yes, sir," replied Tom. "What do you study?" asked Mr. Nielson.

"Engineering," he replied.

"Good!" said John. "A good feller to have around tha fahm!"

As the three men entered through the side door into the kitchen, Annie was at the gas range placing something in the oven. She was dressed in clean denim jeans, a white button-up blouse embroidered with an old-fashioned, red and black flower design. She wore a black and red ribbon in her long blonde hair. She tossed down her pot holders as she swung around to meet the guests. "And this is Annie," said John.

Chris's heart quickened. He dropped his duffle bag on the kitchen floor and held out his hand. "Chris," he said. Annie shook his hand nervously, which bothered her. Her smile broke upon Chris. *Why was she suddenly flushed?*

She saw the fascination in his eyes, and something else—interest, maybe. The only words she could muster were, "I'm roasting a chicken for your supper. It'll be a little late in case you want to fish some this evening, if you're not too tired." She looked to Tom, "Hi!" she said.

"Tom," was all he said, and they shook hands. She quickly glanced back at Chris who was still staring at her, then to her father.

"Okay, fellers," said John, "Let's git the rest of your dunnage."

The three men carried the rest of the gear into the kitchen and John showed the guests some wooden pegs in the molding on the covered porch—a place they could hang their waders to dry when they were "at home". When they were finished John said, "Annie will show you to your rooms." Chris caught himself staring again. Her pretty, green eyes offered their smile. Chris's heart raced again – to his surprise, because his demeanor was usually calm, confident, and alert. He admonished himself for feeling, what was it—*uncoordinated*?

With another radiant grin, Annie grabbed two of the duffels and led the men upstairs. She asked, "Would you like something to eat?"

Tom was about to say "Sure!" but Chris cut him off. "No, thanks, Annie, we'll get right to the river. There should be a caddis hatch in about an hour."

She took them to two bedrooms, small, nicely furnished with fresh bedding, and glass bowls filled with assorted wildflowers and bi-color lupines that were peach with yellow eyes. Chris walked in to the first room and asked, "What kind of lupines are these?"

"Aren't they pretty?" she responded, "Benny Garrison grows them for his landscaping business. Nobody knows where he got them...he can grow just about anything. He's *really* clever. He's even got a greenhouse attached to his cabin."

"Huh." Chris looked back at the flowers and nodded approvingly.

"And you're in here, Tom." Tom also found the lupines in his room and bent down for a long sniff, coming up light-headed.

She was barely down the stairs when Tom exclaimed, "Holy Crap! That girl! She's amazing!"

"Amazing? She's ridiculous! Those eyes! But Thomas—forget her. She's not for you. Let's get ready and go."

Fifteen minutes later, Chris was ready, outside the kitchen door in the late afternoon sunlight.

That evening when Chris and Tom sat down to dinner at the big kitchen table, Annie was quiet, bordering on laconic. After serving apple pie with cream she departed temporarily. "Annie didn't have much to say," said Tom.

"I think she's just being shy," Chris said.

"You know her that well, now?" Both fishermen smiled.

Before long Annie returned and cleared the table. "That was great!" said Chris. Annie smiled, said thanks, and excused herself again.

Chris and Tom retired to the dining room to the big overstuffed chairs and took out the books they had brought for the trip. They avoided the comfortable rocking chair in the corner of the room. It was flanked by a small end table on which there was an ash tray, a pipe and some television remotes. The two were trying to figure out how best to lure Annie into the room and to make her comfortable enough to talk, when John Nielson entered the room, well prepared to engage his visitors with some meaningful conversation.

The young men rose to greet him as Mr. Nielson plunked down in the rocker. "Evenin', boys," he said.

"Is they-ah anythin' you boys want to know 'bout the area?"

"Well, sir, it's Tom's first time to Roslyn, but I've been here fishing many times, and I've talked his ear off about it for a long time. I love it here...always have."

Mr. Nielson waved the air, "Call me John," he said.

"But you could tell us a little what it's like to run a farm these days," said Chris.

There were few topics John Nielson would care to expound on, but that question loosened the farmer's tongue. "Well, it's hahd goin' these days, and that's a fact.

"In the early yeahs Aroostook was a wild county, with only a few roads goin' no-wayah'. Then in the 1800's the Ahmy built some garrisons on account 'o some bordah disputes with the Cannuks and they cut a road all the way t' Fort Kent." John lit his pipe and thought for a moment. "By 1870, Aroostook was covered with fahms. Mostly hay, oat crops and buckwheat. When the railroad finally found its way to Caribou, potatoes took over. Them potatoes came from Peru, ya know." The boys nodded.

John went on. "The few fahms around Roslyn are 'bout as far west as the cleared land got...everythin' else was timber harvestin'. It's tough, here, though. The soil's rocky as hell and the Ph is a bit too high. But when fahmins' in your blood, it's hahd to git rid of.

"The timing's not easy, neithah," he said. "It's a shot period – the hahvest time heeah, that is – not even three weeks. You absolutely have no time to waste.

45

"We've been experimentin' with different crops to make a little more mahgin. Sometimes it cost more to grow the crops than we git for 'em.

"I feel bad 'bout Annie," he said. "Her mom got the cansa and died a few yeahs ago. Now she feels she can't leave the fahm...feels she has to stay and help me. I told her to go, make her own way, but she worries 'bout her old man, I guess. It's a shame if'n ya ask me...top o' her class in school, ya' know."

Chris finally spoke, and as the words left his mouth he realized the question was inappropriate. "What is it Annie would *like* to do with her life?"

John just smiled and tamped out his pipe. "You'll have to ask *her* that, I s'pose." Then John slapped both arms of his comfortable chair.

"I've got t' hit the hay, boys," he said. He stood and turned as though he just remembered something. "There's a story 'bout an old fahmah that won the lottery—over thirty million dollars. When he went to Augusta and got the check, some commissioner asked him, "What are you going to do now with your life?" The fahmah looked down at the check for $30 million and said, "Well...I've been fahmin' for thirty yeahs. Guess I'll keep on fahmin' till the money's gone.

"Night, boys, good luck fishin' tomorrow."

"Good night, John," both men said at once. The boys had given up on the chance to speak with Annie, and figured they might as well turn in also.

At his bedroom door Chris said, "Get some sleep, Tommy boy, and tomorrow we'll rip some lips."

"I'll be happy to hook just one," Tom replied, and with a wave of a hand went into his room down the hall.

Chris had no sooner entered his room when Annie came to his open door with two small snifters of brandy. "Would you care for a nightcap, sir?"

"Annie, darlin'!" He saw her eyes twinkle with pleasure. "That would be perfect!" She handed the brandy to him.

"I'll take Mr. Monroe's to him now," she said.

"Please, don't go – Tom doesn't drink much at all, especially brandy – and please Annie, call me Chris." He looked her in the eye. "You know, you're a superb cook."

"Oh, no...just average, I think." She was blushing.

"You are. Though I wish you had joined us after supper."

"I had to run into town, so I had something to eat earlier. Did my father sit with you?"

"He did...he's an interesting guy."

"May I get you anything else?"

"You're a sweetheart, but I'm all set. Anyway, it's late. You probably want to go to bed."

She blushed at the "sweetheart" and just the mention of her bed. As she walked towards the stairs, Chris watched her slim, athletic shape. He was definitely smitten. The feelings continued to make him feel slightly off balance – a feeling rare for him as a worldly, romantic intellectual. That night he started exploring this strangeness in his heart. It wasn't long for Chris to realize the futility in applying logic to this experience. He had had girlfriends, but he had always kept a healthy distance in those relationships. He reserved his most romantic notions for travel, fly fishing, climbing mountains and learning. He was, a familiar third party might've observed, very much like a young Arno Warren.

Chris tried to catch her as she reached the stairs. "Annie!" he called in a half-whisper. "I want to take Tom to the Blue Moon for breakfast in the morning. Would you like to join us?"

"Can't, thanks," she said. "I've got to help Dad early." Chris was disappointed, but also heartened, for he could see in her face she wanted to go—and would have.

SIX

Tom and Chris slept late the next morning, as planned, because at this time of year even if they got on the river at noon they would be in time for the late morning caddis hatch. At nine-o'clock they ran through their check list to make sure they had everything with them—waders, wading shoes, rods, vests, jackets, landing nets—and then left in the jeep.

"I'll take the long way to the restaurant and give you a quick tour of my town," said Chris. They drove past Doc Warren's place, past the new, half-built log cabin, and past St. Mary's Catholic Church. As they drove past Pelletier's market, he told Tom, "That's one of the places that sells John's produce." They drove past the Baptist church, and past The Riverdriver – the cafe and inn where Chris usually stayed when it wasn't full. When they arrived opposite the pretty cemetery on the hill, Chris pulled to the side of the road and stopped to say hello to Doc and Ennis who were quick-stepping along on their morning walk.

"Long time, no see," said Doc as he snuggled up to the open window, then peered in to the passenger seat. "Hello, Tom. This is Ennis Gray. If you need any flies, or tippet, or feel the need to hear some lies, Ennis owns the Gray's Ghost in town." Tom couldn't reach Ennis to shake his hand, but they gave each other a friendly wave. Doc asked how they fared at the farm. They were engaged in a friendly chat when Doc spotted through the jeep's windows a familiar figure hunched in the walled garden at the front of the cemetery.

"Ah, there's Ben Garrison in the garden," said Doc. All four men looked at the curious shape working the soil in one of the flower beds, kneeling beside flats of marigolds, wave petunias, bacopa and verbena. A small man now in his twenties, he had developed into quite an interesting fellow since Doc had started treating him as a child. He had compensated for the deformities quite well. One arm was slightly thinner than the other and his neck was almost non-existent. Atop his twisted spine sat a remarkably handsome face. He had a perfectly proportioned straight nose, high cheek bones, and alert, attractive gray eyes topped with wavy, light brown hair. The lack of neck length made his head appear too large for his body, but of course it wasn't.

All four men had one similar thought: a pang of sorrow to see such a handsome face on such a misshapen body. It was Annie who once told Doc that if that beautiful face had belonged to a straight, tall body, Benny would be too good to be true.

Arno straightened up and called to him. "Hello, Ben!" and waved. Ben turned, casting a smile which Annie said "could part the clouds on a rainy day."

Chris looked pensive. "Ben Garrison...isn't that the fellow you said was building the log house across from you?"

"Sure is," said Doc.

Chris said, "I wonder how he manages so well, with his deformity, I mean."

"Manages?" interjected Ennis. "He more than manages. He'll probably build a beautiful cabin, though I don't know why he's putting up that cabin when his place on the river is the nicest one in the valley. He's also an amazing gardener, and can do just about anything else. He can hang drywall, run electrical wiring, and build a dry stone wall – which is a dying art, you know."

Doc said something in French to Ben, who answered in English, "Yes, Arno...I've got maybe four more flats, some tall, and some short. I could bring some over to you this afternoon."

"Great," replied Doc, "I'd like to get the window boxes done."

"He speaks French?" asked Chris.

"Oui," said Doc, "and some German, *and* he has some working Latin, also. There's hardly a book in town Ben hasn't read; all of mine, all the books at both the churches, and this time of year he goes to rummage sales to look for books. He collects them...has all his life. A few winters ago he read all the volumes of the 1937 *Encyclopedia Britannica*. Spent the month of March going over maps and charts and studying how the world has changed."

Ennis piped in, "He repaired my pipes two months ago when they froze, too. Oh, and he's my best tier at the shop. His flies have the most amazing detail."

"*Really*?" said Chris, turning again towards Ben.

"Well, we better get going. Breakfast awaits!" said Chris.

"Nice meeting you, Tom," said Ennis.

"You, too; we'll stop by the fly shop when we get off the water."

****

Chris and Tom arrived on the water around 11:30. They were late, but not too late. They parked the jeep off the side of the road past where Lewis Brook joins the river, where the powerline crosses the road overhead. There are turnouts along the river, and here the gravel shoulder is worn thin from years of fishermen pulling off the main road. You can get far enough off the road to be safe. You can't see the water from there, but you're close enough that you know it's there.

They both changed into their waders, put on their boots, strung up their rods, tied on new tippets, and tried to pee before pulling up the suspenders and putting on their fly vests. They walked down through the rough trail towards the water's edge, walking in the soft, spongy ground covered with moss and moose shit. The last hundred feet were down a steep slope. Filtered light from the cedars bathed their approach to the riverbank.

Chris was the first to get close enough to see the river through the trees. He was crouching, trying to see as Tom caught up to him. Chris turned and stared at Tom with a broad, excited smile, "Do you *see* that?!" Tom peered through the branches.

The intense, golden sunlight was unobstructed directly over the river. A few more steps and Tom could see the sight all fly fishermen dream of all winter long; insects by the thousands flittering around over the water, their gauze-like wings highlighted by the sunlight. Some were very near the surface, some twenty feet high. A majority of the flies were moving deliberately upstream, but some were scattering willy-nilly, as though they were drunk on springtime.

This was a section of the West Branch that was only 80 to 120 feet across, punctuated with big boulders and pieces of ledges sticking into the water from the banks. It was a section popular with fishermen because one can find some places to stand waist-high in the water and make most casts count for something. The West Branch of the Penobscot is big water, and there are many parts of it that are unwadeable. There have been drownings in that river, of fishermen and of riverdrivers, back when Roslyn was a lumber and pulp town.

Chris looked upstream, and Tom, to his right, looked down the river. Fish were rising here and there along some of the seams of current in both directions. Tom was only in his second year of fly fishing (he had been pushed to try it by Chris), and was nearly beside himself. In fact, except for a few occasions of catching a glimpse of a few fish rising, he had never seen a full-blown hatch, let alone several hatches at one time. Chris jabbed the amazed Thomas with his elbow, "Welcome to Northern Maine," he said softly, with a wink. "Try not to snap off too many flies." The grassy ground they stood on was a jutting finger of river bank, about five feet above the waterline that extended downstream about forty feet, gradually tapering into the river like a natural ramp. Directly opposite where they stood was a large boulder at least four feet out of the water, and thirty feet farther out from that was an obvious current about ten feet across with fish rising on its far side. It was a good place to fish.

Chris pointed upstream. "You go ahead and start first, Tom. Sneak down this ramp where you can ease into the water, then work your way back up here, just downstream from this big rock. You'll want to get your cast about ten or twelve feet above those rises."

Tom nodded.

"There are a few Olives here and there – there's one (Chris pointed); see...above the big rock? But I think the best bet is a caddis. They're pretty thick right now, and these rises are "soft" like they're taking them in the surface film. Try one of these Elk Hair Caddis, or an Olive Klinkhammer...you choose."

Tom tied on one of the Klinkhammers.

"Two things to remember," Chris said. "Try not to make a lot of wake or splashes wading in here, and right after you make your cast you'll need an upstream mend in your line, okay?"

Tom gave him a thumbs-up and snuck down the bank. Chris watched as he followed the instructions perfectly. He had a moment to gaze around and could see a good size fish rising next to a small boulder about forty yards upstream.

Tom found his footing below the boulder. He payed out some line, gave the leader one more gentle stretch to remove some of its memory, flicked the rod tip and let the line float downstream a short distance. When all the line he had taken off the reel was in the water, he made his first cast; a simple raise of the rod tip, a gentle haul with his left hand, a roll cast downstream got the entire line airborne, but before the line hit the water, Tom turned his body quartering upstream and the roll cast became the actual back cast. Then a deliberate forward cast upstream placed the fly in a perfect position, eight or nine feet above the rises across from him. Immediately, before he could make an upstream mend, the quick water that ran between him and the seam where the trout were rising grabbed the fly line, pulled it downstream, and dragged the fly with it in such an unnatural drift the fish never gave it a thought.

Tom, frustrated, looked over at Chris.

"Two mends!" he whispered. Tom nodded again. "Like you're changing a tire, and you're taking off a nut with a lug wrench. Twist your right hand to the left; the fly line will flick upstream."

Tom made the same cast as the first, but this time he made the mend before the current took the line. It was better. For about five feet the fly floated drag-free, but Chris was right; it needed two mends. This time he made three false casts (too many, as far as Chris was concerned), but when the fly landed it was in perfect position again. This time, he made two successive mends upstream. The fly floated quietly. Tom raised the rod tip as much as he could without pulling the fly out of position, just barely inside the feeding lane. This also was an effort to keep the current from catching the floating fly line and thus dragging the fly. There was a lot going on there, but it was all working.

From where Chris was, high on the bank, he could see the take. He imagined the fly catching the fish's eye. He saw the trout make a deliberate turn, follow the Klinkhammer for a couple of feet, and then swirl and hit it from the side. And when his nose broke the water with a small splash, Tom saw it and gently raised the rod tip while simultaneously pulling a small haul on the line with his left hand, stripping a few inches of line between his right index finger and the rod handle. It was a wonderful hook-set. "That's him!" yelled Chris.

"Yeah!" Tom was excited. The fish thrashed and then ran upstream. Tom put gentle pressure on him to steer him towards his side of the river. It worked, and within a couple of minutes Tom had him in the slack water behind the big boulder, just below his feet. He netted him, a plump fifteen-inch brookie. Chris got a little closer and took their picture.

Tom was like a twelve-year-old kid. He had worked hard for that trout. He had made a difficult cast, and had done everything right. He was content enough to go home, but they didn't. They decided to fish together the rest of that day and they both caught several more fish, including an eighteen-inch salmon Chris caught on a small green caddis pupae pattern with a black head, but that fifteen-inch brook trout was the largest brookie either one caught. All in all, Tom's best day fishing, ever.

It was nearly dark when the boys changed out of their waders and drove back into town, and again Chris's thoughts turned to Annie; *this is ridiculous.*

Having given Tom the tour of the town, Chris took the more direct route to the Nielsons'.

"I could eat a horse," said Tom.

"Well, we are staying at a farm. I'll see what I can do," replied Chris.

As they said this they sped around a corner and Chris suddenly slowed down.

"Look at that!" cried Chris. Snuggled between the road and the river was a stunning little log cabin, low to the ground with a green shingled roof and yellowish, oiled logs. Chris slowed down more and both men were silent for a moment. There was a circular drive, and all they could see was the street side of the building that was in the shade of some big balsams and two pretty cedars. There was a window box for each window, filled with brightly colored begonias. They were past the house by the time they caught glimpses of some gardens. Open land stretched behind the cabin down to the river.

"I wonder if that was that landscaper's place the doctor was talking about," asked Tom. "They weren't kidding when they said it was the prettiest place around. That's like a dream house."

Chris had admired that cabin on previous trips, but never knew who owned it.

"Garrison's..." said Chris. "It has to be."

SEVEN

Ben Garrison sat inside the cabin at his kitchen table reading *Nansen: The Explorer* by Edward Shackleton, one of many books in his cabin about exploration. For several months Ben had had an ongoing debate with Doc Warren about who really got closer to the North Pole, Frederick Cook or Robert Peary. Doc held the convention that it was Peary, while Ben, in his extensive research had concluded that Cook was much closer, close enough by the contemporary instrumentation to lay the claim, but Ben believed Cook was publicly denounced because Peary was sponsored and underwritten by the wealthy industrialists and trust babies of the National Geographic Society. The political juggernaut from the Society actually ruined Cook's life in the long run.

The extensive reading Ben had done about the Arctic had led him to a number of great explorers of the region, some looking for the North Pole, some for the Northwest Passage, and some who went searching for those intrepid souls lost in the beautiful, barren arctic wastelands. Fridtjof Nansen quickly became a sort of hero to him.

Unbeknownst to Ben, Doc was actually on board with the theory of Cook's attainment of the Pole, but relished the ongoing conversations with the young man. Doc loved to see the young man grow. He loved the melody of the conversations, and the art of the debate. Ben was no intellectual slouch. Fairly early on in the discussions, he had found while looking through Doc's library for more literature on the Arctic, an old pamphlet stuffed amongst the books about Nansen, Franklin and Greely. In the pamphlet was Doc's past membership in the Frederick Cook Society – an organization dedicated to forwarding the cause of Cook's claim to the Pole.

When the Cook/Peary debate had finally run its course, the two immediately picked right up with discussions about the quest for the Northwest Passage. They spent most of one summer reclaiming an antique rose garden next to Doc's office, and while they worked, they discussed the ill-fated Franklin expedition of 1845, when both ships the *Erebus* and the *Terror* were lost along with the entire expedition complement of 128 men. Doc debunked the idea that lead poisoning from the solder of food tins (a new technology at the time) or from lead-lined food and water storage containers killed the men, or deranged them enough to make some odd, fatal decisions. (Doc once said that a little lead poisoning wouldn't kill the average British explorer of the mid-nineteenth century, unless the lead was .625 caliber and was traveling at 1000 feet per second.) He maintained that it was the *arrogance* of the nineteenth century explorers that destroyed the expedition. Their disdain for aboriginal people all over the world disallowed them learning anything useful from the Inuit, whom they looked down upon from their ships' decks, regarding them as mere savages. Doc felt if the officers had taken the time – or possessed the attitude – to learn from the native population they might have acquired some survival skills. Ben was a remarkable thinker, and he and Doc never stopped pushing each other intellectually. The ethos of discovery enlivened both men.

Reading about Nansen by the golden light of the propane lamp above the kitchen table, Ben imagined himself an explorer, overcoming all manner of deprivations, pushing himself to the greatest physical limits, and beyond. He imagined the glory and success, and the humble retreat from praise. In his dreams he was always tall, straight and symmetrical with a perfect, sound body.

But Ben's body wasn't straight, or perfect, and never would be...not to him or to anyone else. The awful truth was that in his body were needs no weaker than in those young men who worked in the woods, or in those athletic guides who came to Roslyn each spring. It had always been Annie Nielson who caught his eye. For many years it was impossible for him to look without hunger at Annie, whether she was passing in the street, stopping by his greenhouse for seedlings, or working in her father's kitchen when he would go to the farm to help her father. He always drew pleasure from seeing her slim, withdrawing figure, and he felt no less pleasure from it than did the other men in town, but Ben had to suppress the notion that he felt so much more than desire. His pleasure always quickly turned to pain. His great desire was Annie, no less – the sexiest, most beautiful woman in the valley—and he, a limping cripple. Ben also secretly prided himself on his intelligence, and he knew deep down that he could make someone a wonderful husband, given the chance.

This morning Ben had dropped off some trays of squash seedlings for her father, and he had seen her in the kitchen doorway, laughing and talking with the handsome sport who Doc said was from a wealthy "but nice" family from upstate New York. He had seen her body language as she looked at him, and the old familiar pain swept into his heart. Ben had seen the local boys flirt with her for years, and though his pain was there, he felt she would never settle for one of them. Sure they were good guys, most of them, and might provide a nice life for her, but Annie wanted more. She wanted to travel, and if she couldn't travel physically she would at least travel intellectually—she wanted to learn, study, try new things—she needed to *grow*. And that was exactly what Ben had to offer her – along with the unconditional love he held for her since childhood. He never tried to tell her how he felt. Annie's feelings, her wellbeing, her happiness, always came before his. Another man more fit and more *straight* would better complete the picture of a perfect couple.

It wasn't a matter of finances. The rumor around town had always been that Ben, while living his silent, industrious, solitary life had amassed a small fortune, at least by Roslyn standards. He had resigned himself to a life of deprivation. He had often tossed the line from a song by The Band around in his head: "There's no love as true as the love that dies untold."

He was trying to study, but couldn't concentrate. What if Annie fell in love with the handsome sport? What if the young man took advantage of her adoration and, having enjoyed it, disappeared, only to explore other rivers each spring. This thought made the pain worse, like a knife wound in his heart. He closed the books, and tried to pray, in his own way, for Annie. Ben was perhaps one of the more spiritual individuals in the valley, yet he had never attended church. Morality can be lost or forgotten in the heart of a starved love. Ben's beautiful little cabin had, over time, become more than a hermitage; it became a place where he could explore who he was, who his God was, and what duty meant to him. It became a dwelling of an anchorite. Ben had, in his simple, studious life discovered what his religion was. It was in the river, and the soil, and in the trees. It was in his fellow man. He had learned much from his reading, but some part was derived from an awareness of the body in which he dwelled, an unworthy body.

He felt that the entire material world, from which he took so little, was really made up of something not material, but an eternal, timeless goodness. In this sad, lonesome world in his cabin on the river, his deformity mattered less. He had chosen his own course in life. He resolved to stay that course—one of benevolence, learning, kindness and doing for others. This evening he was employing all his resources to combat the ache of an impossible love, and to keep his feet on his selfless path.

Ben opened a bottle of '86 Penfold's Grange Hermitage, his favorite Australian wine and poured a glass. He took it onto his back deck overlooking the river, and slumped into one of the two Adirondack chairs he had built himself. He had numerable successes helping others in need in his community throughout the years, but now, as usual, he failed to temper his own heartsickness. The prayers didn't help. What remained was only his will. He listened in the darkness to the gentle song of the river's current, and thought of Annie and that athletic good-looking man, and surrendered.

He finished his wine and went back into the cabin. He surveyed his bookshelves on every wall, he looked at the old comfortable chairs that sat in front of the stone mantle above the fieldstone fireplace, and the little antique table in the kitchen. He couldn't help but think: *You'll always be alone. It will never change.*

The only one you'll ever want, you'll never have. You'll find a lesser happiness, in other places.

Ben was not only fond of good wines, but he and Doc were also foodies, and he had become something of a gourmet in the past few years. He decided to prepare a nice meal, to take his mind off things. He placed the book about Nansen away on the shelf in a section with many other books about explorers. Next he prepared a perfect place setting. Then in the efficient little kitchen he started a small pot of basmati rice. He cubed some chicken, and browned the pieces in olive oil with some crushed garlic, the same garlic he grew every year and sold to most of the area restaurants. When the chicken was browned enough he removed it from the pan and placed it aside. He added some chopped leeks and mushrooms to the garlic and sautéed them. While they were cooking he warmed a tortilla in the oven. He turned the sauté pan down low, and in a third small pan he placed a handful of crushed almonds, a bit more garlic and a pat of butter. He toasted the almonds and added a half cup of white wine. Once it had reduced by about half, he added a little sugar to take the bitterness out of the wine. When it tasted good enough for him, he added some heavy cream, then some salt and pepper. The sauce simmered for a few minutes while Ben filled the tortilla with the sautéed vegetables and the chicken. He folded the tortilla into a square, placed it onto a plate with the rice and poured the almond sauce over the burrito.

Then he poured another glass of wine, and sat down to a supper for one.

At the Nielson farm, Chris and Annie were alone. Their dining was finished, and so was the cleaning up. She was still in the kitchen, puttering about, and

Chris sat reading in the living room. Tom, who had recently entered into the unfamiliar territory of fitness, had gone for a long jog. After an uncomfortable wait, Annie went to check on Chris. She was surprised to see Chris staring at the entrance to the kitchen, as if he'd been waiting for her. Her heart raced.

"Annie," Chris said softly, "Are you going to come talk to me, or not?"

"Of course, I'd love to." She wasn't lying. She had been trying to think of a reason to go to him without seeming too anxious.

He stood when she entered the room, and then threw himself back into the comfortable chair. *My God, she's beautiful*, he thought.

Annie sat down in the adjacent chair. She sat upright and attentive. She didn't slump.

"Tom's gone for a run, I guess you know that."

She smiled, and nodded.

"He's a natural athlete, but has never worked out much," said Chris, "He only started fly fishing last fall...he's picking it up fast. Do you fly fish, Annie?" he asked.

"I've threatened to learn for some time," she said. "Ben Garrison has told me he would teach me anytime, but I always seem to be too busy. Sometimes when I'm riding my bike on the river road, I'll stop and watch the fishermen cast for what seems like hours. It's so pretty to watch."

Chris had nothing against Ben. In fact, he was rather intrigued by the young local gardener/angler/fly tier, but *his* dream of Annie included her casting a fly, and loving it.

"Would you come with me, sometime? I'd love to teach you, and I bet you'd pick it up in just a few minutes."

"I'd love to!" Annie said, not giving any thought to the years of offers by Ben to teach her. "But I don't know if I have the time, really, at this time of year." She paused as if considering it carefully. "I hear you fishermen talking all the time, and it seems like an awful lot to learn in just a few minutes."

"You mean the Latin names," said Chris. He couldn't help but stare at her perfect, high but subtle cheekbones, and how they framed her stunning green eyes.

"Latin! Ugh...I took Latin my junior year and hated it! I'll learn to cast, but I'm not learning Latin," she insisted.

Chris chuckled, "Of course not! Most of the fishermen I know don't bother with that garbage, and none of my friends do. When I was a youngster, I learned the scientific names of most of the species of the flies we tie imitations for, but I've forgotten most of them now."

"Doc Warren uses the fancy names," she said.

"Yes, but Doc Warren is a different breed, isn't he?"

"Indeed he is," she shook her head.

Chris was like a preacher, singing the gospel of fly fishing. At times he could work himself into a passionate state, eyes ablaze with the bountiful benefits of casting a fly to a wary trout. When you are on the river, alone with the water and the fish, you could slip away from the world of men, and from their rules and conventions. He was getting serious, so Annie reined him in.

"You love it, I can see that," she said.

Chris blinked and looked at her again, "Love it? Oh yeah, I love it. When you're in the right place on the river, and the sun is stabbing through the cedar branches and the temperature is perfectly comfortable, and you're casting to a pretty pool somewhere, your troubles and your cares have already floated away. You feel as though it's just you and the Creator there. I can tell you, Annie, it can feel damn near perfect. It *can* be better than sex."

Annie blushed, and Chris caught himself and smiled a wry little smile.

"Annie," he said, "do you have a boyfriend?"

She was caught entirely off guard. "That was some segue," she said. She shook her head once. "No. I don't have much time these days, and there isn't much of a dating scene here in Roslyn." She tried to laugh it off, but her eyes showed embarrassment and slight resignation.

"How about you?" Annie asked.

"Oh, God, no...I like girls."

Annie burst out laughing and mock-slapped Chris's shoulder.

"No," he paused for a moment. "I dated most of last year, but I was traveling a lot when I wasn't in school." Another pause, as though he was searching for the right words. "I liked a couple of women, and they liked me, I guess, but it always got complicated."

"How so?" asked Annie.

"Well, even though I was honest with them right from the start, and told them I was traveling a lot, and that I had quite a few trips I had committed to, it seemed like when the time came to go away they really struggled with me being gone a lot. In the beginning of the relationship, they were fine with the idea, but I guess not when it came right down to it.

So I suppose I just stopped dating to obviate the hassles and the stress.

"Travel and fish," said Chris. "Wow! I sound like a selfish bastard when I say that stuff out loud!"

"I'll say!" said Annie.

They both had another laugh, and Chris reached out and gently took Annie's hand. She was startled. It's what she wanted—but again he took her by surprise. They both just looked at each other for a moment, and smiled the smile that sometimes follows a good, hard laugh.

Chris finally spoke. "Knowing all that, Annie, would you go out with me?"

Annie looked into his beautiful, deep-set eyes, beneath his wavy brown hair, charmed by his disarming smile. Instantly she swept aside her earlier trepidation. She forgot about her worries about the class difference – she, a simple Maine rural farm girl, no matter how talented or sharp her mind was – and he, a well-educated, well-traveled man from a wealthy family. She realized in amazement at how comfortable she was with Chris. How comfortable she was with the notion of the two being together, in any way. She sat back in her chair and felt comforted, and looked confidently at Chris, square into his pleasing eyes.

"Of course I will."

They both stiffened when they heard Tom walk up the stairs and go into the hall bathroom for a shower. At the sound of the door closing behind him, Chris squeezed Annie's hand gently and they looked into each other's eyes and smiled—a big smile this time—and Annie said, "I've got to go now. We'll talk tomorrow."

"Goodnight, Annie." And Chris leaned over and kissed her right cheek.

Annie rose and went out the door and down the hall to the stairway leading to the living room. She walked the hallway quicker than usual, her excitement hardly containable. She didn't know it, but Chris was still sitting in the exact same position as she left him, unable to move. She didn't know that Chris was experiencing a defining moment in his life—his exciting, worldly life. She had assumed but wasn't certain that Chris had been with other women, and he was no virgin. And Annie had no idea that as she went into her bedroom, Chris was still slumped in the chair, weighted by the realization that his simple, innocent kiss on her right cheek – meant to be amiable – was in fact the most wonderful, heartfelt kiss of his life. He went to his bedroom and lay on the bed, thinking.

Tom awoke Chris from his stupor when, shirtless, and still drying his hair with a towel after his shower, he went into Chris's room.

"What's wrong?" asked Tom.

Chris looked up at him with a deliberate, acquiescent look and said, "I think I'm in *love*."

Tom cocked his head slightly, pursed his lips, and threw the towel at Ben.

"Well, Christopher, I can't say I'm not flattered."

EIGHT

In the morning, Tom, Chris and Annie sat at the kitchen table having a cup of coffee and engaging in small talk. Tom was, at least. Chris spent most of the time staring at Annie and she at him, both trying unsuccessfully to be inconspicuous.

"What time does your dad start working, anyway?" asked Tom, as he stood up and walked to the window that overlooked the south field.

"He's usually out by 5:30," she replied, "even on the weekends."

Tom turned around and leaned on the counter, drinking his coffee. He looked at Chris, and then at Annie, who were still smiling at each other. An awkward moment passed until Chris realized they were in a conversation with Tom and he caught himself, glancing over at him.

"Sorry, Tom," he said.

"Okay...you guys are starting to creep me out," said Tom.

Annie and Chris both snorted a quick laugh, and Tom took a sip of his coffee, raised his mug toward the two and said, "It's cool. You kids have fun."

"Well," said Chris, "We better get going if we want to hit the hatch."

The boys emptied their coffee mugs into the sink and started out the door. Annie patted Tom on the shoulder as he left, and Chris leaned in to give her another kiss on the cheek, and this time Annie wasn't surprised, she in fact was waiting for it and she kissed him back. It was still on the cheek, but enough of a kiss to lift her off her feet.

As the jeep rolled down the driveway, Annie's mind was reeling. As she sat back down at the little table she thought to herself, *What the Hell am I doing?* It doesn't matter how right it feels, she thought, what did she have to offer someone like him? She was at once the happiest she'd ever been, and yet saddened from worry. She gazed into the coffee cup and saw nothing. Finally Annie looked out the kitchen window and felt once again that old familiar feeling. She was being foolish. She had resigned herself to a life of helping her father keep the farm – at least for a while. When her father had decided the time was right to start letting out rooms, she started daydreaming. Dreams of young guests, of people from away. Dreams of...romance, perhaps? Chris had only served to enlarge the dream. In fact, he had made it real. Anytime a dream becomes reality it can be frightening, if not downright overwhelming. Chris had told her much about his family the night before, of his own dreams, about his travels, and his fears. It was obvious he came from a privileged background. With that foolish feeling, her forty-eight hour high from what she considered to be love at first sight was crashing to the ground. She saw in her reeling mind a beautiful brownstone in Brookline, with an old carriage house and manicured grounds. Then she pictured a run-down farmhouse in a remote part of Maine, in a town, lovely as it is, with one road in and one road out. She should face her life the way it is, she thought, before she falls even more in love, and makes the matter worse.

There were cultural class differences, to be sure. Hadn't she made a case for herself by bragging – ever so slightly – about her successes at school, her college acceptances, and the many books she'd read?

Had she not talked about herself with a certain confidence, and hadn't she mentioned that she might have done well in life if she hadn't chosen to stay and help with the farm? When she went over these things in her mind, she thought, *Oh my God! I was bragging! Social gaffes!* She was never seeking praise or any type of admiration; she was simply trying to stay on somewhat even ground intellectually with Chris, and with Tom, for that matter.

Oh well, she thought, *might as well see how the week goes.* They had made a date for that night. Maybe she could hold in check the notion that she was falling in love with Chris, and just have some fun. She hadn't been on a date for over a year, after all. Perhaps by tonight he'll have forgotten her awful bragging the night before. She hoped he would still like her and they could enjoy their time together before he returned to his world. A world she felt she would never know.

On the way to the river Tom finally broke the silence.

"You got a plan?"

"I don't know, Tom, this girl's got me on my heels. I haven't been able to think of anything except Annie since I met her. Hell, except for my plan to teach her to cast, I haven't even thought about fishing for two days."

Tom, alarmed, looked at Chris. "Seriously? I've never seen you like this – not with any girl. You're scaring me."

"That's because I've never met a woman like this. And a plan? No, there's no plan."

"Well, she's the most beautiful girl I've ever seen," said Tom,

"It's not just that, there's *something*, I don't know...a quality about her. You see it, don't you?"

"Yup," said Tom. They arrived at the parking spot for the bend pool they wanted to try. Usually Chris was rigged up and in his waders before Tom (or anybody else, for that matter) could put his reel on his rod, but today Tom finished first.

They walked down the short, steep path, and stepped out onto the big boulders that lined the bank.

"Right on time," said Chris. The overcast sky was filled with beige-colored caddis flies fluttering every which-way, looking as though they'd been drinking, and had suddenly been called to flight. Usually Chris would take some time, observe the water's surface, and poke through the streamside foliage before actually making a cast. In his younger years, he was more casual in his approach, and would wade right in and begin fishing upon arrival, but had learned the advantage of being patient from Doc Warren when the two had fished together some years earlier. Today he offered the first cast to Tom, but instead of wandering upriver or down to fish, Chris just plunked down on a convenient boulder, and watched the river go by.

He was thinking; about Annie, about his life, about Roslyn and now, about home and his family. He had always been a confident, smart, capable guy, who always seemed in control of his destiny. A week ago, he was contemplating his immediate future: soon to have his degree in finance, perhaps intern with his father trading stocks, maybe a master's degree after a sweet fishing and climbing trip to Europe. Now, things were suddenly different. Now there was Annie. Was he crazy? He had to wonder. Could he ditch his opportunities and live with Annie in Roslyn? It was his favorite town in the world, but his parents would probably disown him. Was that too harsh a thought? His father would probably come around after some time, but his mother! His mother would surely be disgusted with him. What about Annie? If she would have him, would she move with him, and leave her father and Roslyn behind? He knew he was being silly, dreaming about such things so soon after getting to know Annie. *Jumping the gun,* he said to himself. The problem was, Annie was the girl of his dreams. He knew it the instant he met her. And, sitting on that rock, watching the river run, and ignoring the caddis flies and the salmon rising in the pool below him, he accepted it.

Tom caught and released two nice salmon in the bend pool without Chris even noticing. When he felt the pool was tired, he waded back to the bank to try another spot. He started downriver along the narrow path below the boulders when Chris called to him.

"We have to be careful just downstream!" he said loudly enough to be heard over the roar of the river. Below the bend pool was a thousand-yard stretch of Class IV rapids...white water with one to two-foot standing waves littered with protruding boulders, eddies and plunges that could be deadly for anybody who might have fallen overboard from one of the frequent rafts that went through, and certain death for a fly fisher with no flotation device, who's waders would fill with water. There were fish in there, alright, and big ones have been caught from that stretch, but it was particularly hard to fish.

"Tom!" Chris cried again.

Tom stopped, turned and waited for Chris, now working his way down from the boulders.

"I was beginning to wonder if you were going to fish at all today," Tom smiled, "I got three on that bead-head pheasant tail nymph we bought at Ennis's shop."

Chris didn't smile back, which injected a certain seriousness to the conversation. "Below here is the big water I told you about. There are only a couple of places you can safely fish from, so we better go on down together." Chris was practically yelling to be heard over the boiling rapids not six feet away. Chris's face bore the signs of concern. It was pretty clear to Tom that this section of the river deserved more respect than normal.

God, Chris thought to himself, *Annie's got me completely unfocused.* He might as well have said it out loud... Tom knew exactly what was on Chris's mind at this point.

Here the river rolled down a six percent grade for a quarter-mile before it dropped into the valley above Millinocket. It could be dangerous. If an angler took a dunk in the frothy water, there would be no branches or rocks to hold on to—there would be nothing. The water was too deep and too heavy to swim, and the angler would be dragged under water and pummeled through the hundreds of boulders. The body would eventually be deposited by the river when it was done with it into one of the eddies or bend pools, or maybe lost forever. Everyone in Roslyn had heard the stories of the two river drivers in the old days that drowned one spring. Not twenty feet from where Chris and Tom stood, a log jam had broken loose and crushed the men's legs before pulling them under.

Where the River Road comes close to the water next to the flats below the rapids, there are two graves along the gravel shoulder, and the drivers are supposedly buried there. Some variations tell the tale as the drivers were brothers, some say they were friends. Either way, both graves are hardly five feet long from head-to-toe, and although men were shorter 130 years ago, most local people think someone just made some rough graves there ages ago to perpetuate the legend. Over the years, the stones and markers have become something real.

"There are three spots you can cast from safely," said Chris, still loudly, and pointing at one piece of rock ledge protruding out into a succession of standing waves. "When the water's low enough, you can walk out onto that ledge and make an upstream cast, but you have to mend the line quickly, two or three times to get any drift at all. Now Tom, you have to watch the water level! If it rises quickly, you'll have a hard time getting back to the bank."

Tom nodded, indicating he understood.

"It looks low enough now, if you want to try it," yelled Chris.

Tom side-stepped through the alders and worked his way onto the first part of the ledge. It was wide enough here by the bank, but it narrowed as it tapered out into the whitewater, about forty feet from shore. On the upriver side, the water smashed into the granite ledge in a relentless but shallow torrent; the downriver side was another matter. There the entire length of the sliver of ledge was a sharply sloped slide of rock descending into a deep eddy, and a swirl of strong moving current, drove itself counter clockwise along the ledge where it rejoined the main rapids of the river. Tom moved carefully. He could see that Chris was right. One wrong step and he could slide down the rock and into the eddy. It was definitely too deep to touch bottom, and there would be nothing to grab onto. And the current—if his waders filled with water, there was surely enough power in the eddy to deposit him into the rapids. It was dicey.

It wasn't hard to walk on the ledge; the surface was pocked with small, smooth ridges, left by the insults from the relentless water. But Tom still had to be careful. It would be all too easy to turn an ankle, or worse, slip downriver into the eddy. Even though he was walking on dry ledge, he felt the need to use his walking staff.

Once out to the end of the ledge, Tom placed his feet in two of the shallow depressions in the granite. From this position he could make a balanced cast. Chris still stood on the bank watching intently. Standing on the rock, his feet wide apart, Tom surveyed the river. It was big water. The main current rumbled by about twenty-five feet in front of him. There was a nice feeding lane along the edge of the rapids, but it was on the opposite side from him. Tom looked around to see if Chris was still around, and got a "thumbs up" and a wave of an arm to the left, as though he was making an imaginary reach cast. Tom nodded in acknowledgement.

A reach cast isn't hard to do, but it can look like shit. Tom payed out some line and made a few false casts until he had about forty feet on fly line in the air. When he had the spot selected to place the nymph, quartering upstream across the big current, he was ready. On the final forward cast, just as the fly line was starting to unroll, he made a deliberate reach with his arm and rod to the left and tossed the line upstream. The fly hit the water a little downstream from the fly line, but not enough. The current ripped the cream-colored fly line downriver before Tom had time to make a single mend. He picked up the line quickly and after two more false casts he tried again, this time with a left hand reach so dramatic that he almost fell over. It startled him— falling left, upstream, wouldn't be a big deal—to the right would be catastrophic.

Again the current ruined the drift, and again he tried, and again he failed. He was still struggling with his footing somewhat, and decided to pack it in before he fell and broke his fly rod. As he climbed back on shore he shrugged to Chris.

"Tough cast," he said, "tough footing, too."

"No doubt!" said Chris. "Good try, though...I wouldn't have done anything different. There's some nice salmon in that run, if a guy can get to 'em. Let's go back upstream and fish the Warden's Pool."

Tom was puzzled, not because of the complex casting problem he had just tried to solve, but because Chris had yet to wet a line and he'd never seen him in such a state.

NINE

The Warden's Pool didn't look like anything spectacular; in fact, it didn't look like a pool at all. It was more a run, with a nice feeding lane along a medium-fast current below some boulders. The casting was easy and so was the access. It held both salmon and trout consistently. Over time it had become known as the warden's pool because it could be observed from a truck parked next to the road, but the truck couldn't be seen well from down on the river.

As the visitors parked the jeep in the warden's parking spot, they noticed someone already fishing from the choicest rock. He was alone, and he was a beautiful caster. Chris took his binoculars from the console. "Man! Look at that rhythm." Tom could only see the motion of the angler, and a hint of the fly line, shimmering in the sunlight as it unfurled behind him. But Chris could see quite clearly through the glasses the efficiency of the fisherman. He could see that he was a young man, but he cast his fly with a gentle, poetic measure. Chris noted the economy of effort like the old men he would watch fish the trout streams in the Catskills. In his childhood during summer vacations, the old timey fishermen would arrive at the brooks and streams on weekdays, and spend at least as much time sitting and smoking their pipes as fishing.

That's how this guy was fishing, with his casting arm tucked to his side, with a gentle forward stroke and a nice, tight loop. He was a little hunched over, as though he was trying to see the fly on the water but it was out of his focal length. Chris watched as the angler hooked a fish, played it perfectly and then, when he reached down to release the salmon, he could see through the binoculars a back brace protruding out from under his fly vest.

"Two bits says that's the fellow who owns that cool cabin upriver...you know, the same guy building the cabin in town," said Chris. "We met him with Arno."

"*Two bits?* Who says two bits anymore?" replied Tom. "What *are* two bits, anyway?"

"Twenty-five cents," said Chris, still peering through his binoculars. "Let's go say hi and then fish our way upstream."

As they climbed down the path and over the rocks and gravel to the bank where Ben Garrison was fishing, Chris spoke up with a "Hello!" so as not to startle him. Ben turned and gave the fellows a little nod of the head and a smile. He was fishing wet, wearing only wading shoes and shorts, and the cold water didn't seem to bother him any. Ben immediately started reeling in.

"We were just going to head upriver," said Chris, concerned they were crowding Ben.

"I was getting ready to quit, anyway," said Ben.

Tom was already working his way up the trail, and Chris waited by the bank. He had become intrigued by this man who was a master gardener, fly tier, log cabin builder, and who knows what else.

"It's Ben, right?" Chris held out his hand and Ben shook it tentatively.

"Yes sir."

"You're a heck of a caster," said Chris.

"Thanks to Arno," was all Ben said, trying his best to smile and to be engaging.

"Well," replied Chris, "I've fished with Doc for quite a few years, and he doesn't cast as pure and effortlessly as you do."

Ben was embarrassed now, for he wasn't used to the compliments or attention. "I fish a lot," was all he could muster.

The two talked, as two men of some accomplishment will sometimes do, when they meet alone in their shared field of expertise. They sized each other up in a surreptitious way while keeping a congenial conversation going, quite a job when one participant is Ben. Chris marveled at Ben's 5-weight cane rod with the pretty dark green windings around the delicate guides. He noticed how light it felt in his grip. He was astonished to learn that Ben had built the rod himself, admitted reluctantly, with a modest shrug. They talked about the hatches over the last few days. They talked about the water level, and about fly tying. Chris was good enough at engaging people that he never noticed that Ben was almost monosyllabic. Yet, Ben's keen mind was clearly apparent. Chris liked him and was intrigued by him. He noticed Ben's back brace and had to stop himself from asking about it. While Chris enjoyed their conversation, Ben stood in one spot, leaning a little to the left for the entire time, inwardly uncomfortable. When he heard Tom back up on the road loading his gear into the jeep, Chris asked if Ben would like to join them in town for supper. Ben, taken by surprise, awkwardly said he couldn't, that he had "a prior engagement".

With that they shook hands and Chris walked up the steep path to the jeep, broke down his gear and drove off. Ben stood by the river waiting for them to leave before walking up the trail to the road. Chris was likeable enough, he thought, but by now the gossip tongues were wagging. Although he was not plugged into the gossip pipeline, even he knew there was something between Annie and Chris, and that image was painful. As he watched the jeep round the bend out of sight, he knew that Chris would soon be with Annie. *His* Annie, the woman he had dreamt of night and day, whom he had longed for these many years, the woman he loved in vain and always would. His throat hurt a little.

On the way back to the Nielsons', Chris pulled off to the side of the road in front of the old cemetery. "Check this out," he said. "It'll only take a moment."

Chris led Tom along the left-hand side of the narrow, half-circle dirt road through the graveyard.

"Don't tell me you've already purchased a spot!" said Tom.

"No, but I can't think of a better spot than this to be buried...not a legal one, anyway."

In the back left corner of the cemetery were the graves of two young fishermen who had drowned years before.

"I've researched them," said Chris, still staring down at the headstones. "They were friends, one local, the other from Portland, and they fished together every summer. Their canoe capsized just above where we fished today. Neither one could get to shore and they were bashed by the rocks. But this poor guy (pointing to the grave on the left) had lost his girlfriend a few years earlier in a car wreck, and was never the same. Fishing was all he had left."

Tom looked solemnly at the headstone.

George Longley
Died
May 13, 1963
Age 27 yrs.
Died while fishing with his best friend, and now lies by the river he loved.

The parents had added a single line along the bottom of the stone: *Why should we ask here long to stay, Since those we loved have passed away.* "Some parents," said Chris.

Tom and Chris came away from the graves quietly, and as they reached the gate by the road they saw Annie coming across the street with a bag of groceries.

"Hello, you two!" she said. "Pretty little cemetery, isn't it?"

"Beautiful!" said Chris. "I bet people are dying to get in there!"

Annie and Tom rolled their eyes simultaneously. "Would you like a ride to the house, beautiful?" asked Chris.

Annie blushed a little—she was blushing a lot these days. "It's so lovely out, and I don't want to get home too early, I guess I'd rather walk. You won't be offended, will you?"

"Only if you don't let me walk with you," he replied.

Tom saw it coming, and was already reaching for the grocery bag. "I'd like to stop at the fly shop for something anyway. I'll meet you kids at the house."

"Keys are in it," said Chris, and Tom gave him a salute and a smile as he got to the driver's side door.

Annie stood smiling at Chris as the jeep drove off. "So...let's walk," he said, smiling back.

They closed the gate behind them, and as they started walking Ben Garrison drove by in his lovingly restored 1965 International Harvester Scout 80. He saw the happy pair walking along the road, laughing and talking together, one of them that tall, athletic young sport. The pains came back in an instant. He had dawdled by the river and thought for sure he had given the men enough time to get to where they were going so he wouldn't run into them again. As he watched them walk, he saw the man reach out and take hold of Annie's hand. They swung their arms in affectionate fun, exactly the way he had imagined *he* would be with Annie, if he were able. Ben turned down Lincoln Street toward his in-town building project. He wanted to put up the last course of logs while it was still light enough. He did not look back at the couple again. He just muttered to himself, *know my place*. It was what he said when hopelessness filled his heart. He had said that over the years so many times that it had become automatic.

At the very moment of Ben's anguish, Annie was speaking of him to Chris; after Chris had told her about the meeting he and Ben had had earlier on the river. Annie said, "Isn't he one of the most handsome men you've ever seen? Everybody loves Ben, but it's so sad having a face like that on a crippled body."

"Crippled!" said Chris, "I don't see that he's crippled at all."

"You don't?"

"Not at all; look, I can see the neck and shoulder malformation, and his back is bent, but put those three things in here for a moment (he cupped his hands together as if holding a little bird). Just look at everything he is; he's strong as an ox, and he's capable of so many worthwhile things it's crazy. I think he's gifted and talented, and you know what else? I think he's a natural athlete."

Annie was amazed.

"You know what else?" he went on. "I bet if he hadn't been born with whatever it is that stunted his bones, he would be the handsomest, most sought-after, king-jock in town, and he'd either gone off to college or left this town. Or he'd be working in the woods or driving a logging truck right now, and maybe he wouldn't know how to cook, or be an amazing gardener, or fly rod builder, or angler, or mechanic, or whatever all else he is. Maybe, Annie, he'd be married to the most beautiful woman to ever grace Roslyn." He looked at her from the corner of his eye.

Annie looked at Chris, then at the sidewalk. How could Chris pick up on so much about her extraordinary old friend in such a short time? He was so insightful; she wanted to do as he asked. She held the deformities to the side. In her mind's eye, she thought of Ben; she pushed away his strange-shaped neck, his bent back, and his limp. Suddenly, his neck looked normal. His back looked muscular, and his limp looked almost like he was walking and slightly dancing at the same time. And she saw Ben's face, those wonderful deep-set eyes, his perfect hair, his well-defined chest and muscular arms, and his perfect shaped butt that (now that she was thinking about him this way) is pretty damned nice! She was still walking and thinking when she heard Chris mutter something.

"Excuse me?" she asked.

"Oh, I was just remembering an old quote, *"uva uvam videndo varia fit."*

"Which is?" she said.

"It's Latin, an old proverb used by different cultures. It means something like *grapes* (or plums) *get their color by looking at another.* Depending on which culture you get it from, its meaning can be translated different ways, like *one bad grape spoils the bunch* as in, one rotten *apple.* Another translation is roughly, *we are changed by the lives around us.* But I was just thinking now how it's apropos for Ben Garrison. I make my own translation of that proverb – and I know it's wrong – but it's way better: *grapes become varied grapes through living.* I've never looked up what that would really be in Latin, but it is a lot like Ben Garrison. Think of it. Grapes start out pretty much the same fruit, but throughout their lives – their *living*— they are subjected to different soil, and different pH, unique water perhaps, wind, care, fertilizer...you name it. All these experiences make the grapes come out differently, sometimes vastly different fruit. Products of our environment, you see, at least to a degree."

"With Ben, his anomalies have steered him towards the life he has. Here's a guy who was dealt a shitty hand and has played it deftly. I can tell he's not ever going to let me get to know him, but I'm telling you he is one of the coolest people I've ever met. Have you ever seen him cast a fly?"

"Oh, I've seen him cast," she replied wryly.

"What?" Chris smiled at her.

Annie winced and smiled at the same time. "I can tell you, I guess. For a few years I used to watch him standing in Lewis Brook in hip waders, casting and casting and catching fish, and I would sometimes fantasize that he was tall and straight, and we were married."

"You're kidding," Chris said.

"No! I did!" she said with a laugh. "Is this too weird for you to hear?"

"Absolutely not!" he said. "Actually, it makes me love you more, knowing that you have always seen what a neat guy he is. And his deformities? I don't think they slow him down a bit."

The rest of the way home, there was the normal conversations of young people falling in love, trying to sound interesting, but not pompous or self-important, each trying to get the other person to talk about themselves. It was natural for both of them, so the conversation was easy. But the entire time Annie was thinking about what Chris had said about Ben. She agreed with all of it, and vowed to spend more time with her childhood friend in the near future. Most of what he said about Ben she already knew, but she was seeing him now in a very different light.

TEN

As Chris and Annie strolled up the dirt driveway still holding hands (a rather big deal to Annie) he pulled her to a stop and told her he wanted to say something to her. She smiled a little and bit her lip gently and looked him square in the eyes. "Annie darling," he said, "I've never met anyone like you. I'm so comfortable with you. I know we haven't known each other long at all, but I want to take this to the next step."

Annie recoiled, and gave him one of those "Exactly what do you mean?" looks.

"Annie," he took both her hands in his now, "Tomorrow...I...I want to teach you to fly fish." Annie laughed aloud and slapped his shoulder while he giggled. She wagged a finger at him as she started walking again, looking *very* sexy. "Be careful about squandering golden opportunities!" She glanced back a second time, "They can wither quicker than a rose."

He liked the reference to Houseman. Although he didn't know exactly what she meant by that, he was intrigued. "We'll make plans after supper," he told her.

Chris waved at Tom, who was sitting in an old rocker on the wrap-around porch, his nose in *Hatch Guide for New England Streams*, by Thomas Ames, Jr. Chris joined him, plunking down in an old wicker chair. For a moment neither spoke, then finally Tom did, not looking up from the pages. "Well, you're having quite a little vacation, aren't you?"

Chris smiled and looked out over the farm. "Yup."

That evening after supper, when Chris and Tom sat again on the porch waiting for Annie, it was John Nielson who joined them. "So, boys, how's the fishin' so fah?" he asked.

"Couldn't be better, sir," said Chris a little bummed out. He was glancing around for Annie.

"Annie says you want to take her fishin' tomorrow," said John, lighting his pipe. "I suppose that will be fine, long as you don't put her into any big water. She means everythin' to me. You undastand, don't ya, son?" John looked Chris straight in the eye.

"I will care for her as if she were my own," Chris answered.

John understood that Chris was saying he would teach her in some easy spot, but was still staring at him, wondering what that entailed. After a long, awkward moment, he gave up and said, "Well, I asked her to be back for lunch so she could help me plant the squash seedlings."

******

They stood at the edge of a beautiful pool a few hundred yards up Lewis Brook, where facing the brook there was nothing but grass behind them. Tom started fishing near the road and would work his way upstream to them. Chris first explained the mechanics of the fly rod to Annie, how instead of a piece of hardware flung through the air pulling the fishing line behind it like with a spinning rod, a fly rod throws a line first which then pulls a leader and lure behind it, unfurling it, hopefully, gently onto the water.

He showed her how to hold the rod, how to keep her elbow tucked to her side, and how to not bend her wrist. He then showed her how far to take the rod back during the back cast. He demonstrated the back and then the forward cast, over and over again. He explained that the tip of the rod, about one-third the rod's length, was designed for the cast, not for fighting fish. Then his teaching took a turn.

He seemed to go into a semi trance and as he cast his line back and forth, gently, easily, he said, "You see Annie, the rhythm's the thing. Quite often teachers and instructors make fly fishing way too complicated. It isn't. There are about three basic mechanical things to learn, and the rest is rhythm.

"Think of poetry," he said. "I know you like poetry; I saw you left your *Sonnets from the Portuguese* on the kitchen counter last night. Casting the line, leader and fly is all about rhythm. Poetry, most poetry at least, is based on rhythm and meter, right?" Annie nodded.

"And in nature there is a basic need for rhythm, and we humans feel those rhythms, whether it's the seasons, or the songs of the birds, or in the current of the river. In poetry, the rhythm elicits pleasure or an emotional response from the reader which holds their attention long enough to reward them with beautiful, insightful words – phrases that move them, or reveals something, hopefully something profound. So if you take anything from this lesson, remember that to cast well you have to be patient, and you have to wait for the line to unfurl behind you before starting the forward cast. When you accomplish the rhythm in your cast, you become part of it all.

Annie held the rod just the way Chris showed her. She payed out a few yards of line and stood on the grassy bank facing the brook, holding the rod straight out in front of her, parallel to the ground. She kept thinking to herself, *Elbow in, wrist straight.* She raised the rod quickly and came forward too fast and there was an audible "snap" when the line came forward, and the line fell in a bunch at her feet. Chris laughed softly and said, "Just a bit too quick. Let's try again."

This time Chris touched her back, and said, "Let me help you with the rhythm." He stepped closer to her, from the left and from behind. He gently held her right hand, the cork handle of the rod still in her grasp. He made sure his wrist was bracing hers and he cradled her left forearm in his left hand. She could almost feel him against her from behind, but he was being careful not to lean into her. She could smell the faint smell of the shampoo he used, and she thought for a moment she could feel his breath on the back of her neck. It was physical contact she wasn't used to. It made her nervous, and she liked it.

"Now let's try together," he said, and with that he deliberately swung the rod up to the sky just past perpendicular. Quickly Annie tried to cast back down for the forward cast, but Chris held her arm still while the fly line laid out smoothly behind them. Once it did, Chris pressed her arm down towards the stream where the line, extending from a tight loop, fell softly in a straight line on the water.

"This is a haul," said Chris as he drew the line in with his left hand, pulling it through Annie's right index finger where she held the line close to the rod handle. As he finished the haul, he repeated the same cast, and it was perfect. "The haul takes up any slack in the line and makes the beginning of the cast more efficient." He turned his head toward her as he explained, and this time she was sure she felt his breath on her cheek. She was learning how to cast, no doubt, but all she could think about was kissing this handsome, wonderful man who was teaching her something new – something beautiful, and who was now pressing into her backside. But Chris kept her casting, so that the soft rhythm of a well-executed cast might be imprinted in her memory.

"Sometimes it's helpful to have a little saying or mantra at the top of the cast when you're learning to slow down...to help with the rhythm," he said. "Let's try that." Chris twitched the rod tip and made sure none of the fly line was looped in the guides. He held her hand and the fly line in his left hand, and made a long, deliberate haul. As he did, he guided Annie's right arm up into the "top" position, and the line started flying backward. Just then he whispered in her left ear, "*Quicker than a rose*," then started the forward cast. The timing was perfect. The line laid out from a nice, tight loop and trailed on the water, and Annie blushed, just a little, that he remembered her earlier barb.

"Let's take a break," he said. He didn't notice that she was breathing hard. They sat cross-legged on the grassy bank of the brook in the shade of an old maple tree. "Truth is," said Chris, "fly casting is not as difficult as people think. People think it's hard, but it isn't. And really, I've seen a lot of instructors make it hard, and I don't know why. We've been at it for what...twenty minutes? And you're already getting enough line out – and gracefully enough – to catch a fish."

He told her how the beginner is often tempted to throw out too much line, which only serves as a handicap in learning the cast. He said the purpose of fly casting isn't to see how *far* one can cast, but *where* you can cast, and how you present the fly to the fish. Accuracy, rather than distance is essential to fly casting. "If we're talking about essence," he said, "I suppose the true *essence* of fly casting is a bit different for every angler, but fly fishermen, generally speaking, don't get bummed out about getting skunked like bait fishermen do. Most of the fly fishers I know can spend most of a day on a river just casting, and stay happy. They work on their casting, or the presentation of the fly, or they just enjoy the mechanics of the cast – as if the delivery of the fly is a sport unto itself."

Chris thought for a moment before speaking again. "You said you've watched Ben Garrison cast for long periods of time. Did he ever look frustrated or unhappy?"

She shook her head.

Chris explained, "That's because he's not."

"I've watched him also," said Chris. "When that guy is fishing, whether he's catching fish or not, he's writing poetry on the spot. And when he *is* writing, he's in a different world...like any poet. He's in a world of meter, and rhythm, and freedom. He's in a world that's his own. The next time you get a chance to watch him fish, you'll understand that fly casting is by far the most graceful of all the types of fishing and even the person who knows nothing of fishing can't help but admire the skill and grace of a well-placed cast."

He caught himself. "I'm sure you already know that."

It seemed to Annie that Chris could go on forever about fly fishing, and now she wanted to know everything.

"Fly fishers are a breed apart," he said. "They have their own sense of sportsmanship, which is pretty strict. For instance, if you see some beer cans left littered on a river bank, you can bet the life of your unborn child it wasn't a *serious* fly fisher who left them. And most of the 'Fly Fishing Only' people I know practice catch-and-release...at least a majority of the time. They might on occasion keep one or two to eat, but I don't know one fly fisherman who's ever said, 'Got my limit today.' Personally, I haven't killed a brook trout or a salmon in years."

"Mostly what I'm trying to say, Annie, is that with fly fishing there's never any monotony. Because of the art of the cast, if the fishing is slow, one can find enjoyment in practicing his or her technique...even if there's no fish in that ditch."

"No, I definitely get it," said Annie. "Just in the short time we tried it, I felt what you're saying. And I can see that just like anything else practice will be essential. What I'm more worried about is the language, and learning all the bugs."

"The language?" asked Chris.

"I swear you guys speak a different language when I hear the sports down at the Driver. And your fly boxes...you must have a thousand flies, and I just don't know if I have the time to learn all that."

Chris smiled and put his arm around her shoulders. "That's another thing about fly fishers. We're a pretty democratic lot; we all will go to great pains to help a beginner who shows some interest in the sport. Besides...for me it means spending more time with the most beautiful woman on the planet, and at my favorite place on the planet...on the water."

The most beautiful woman? On the planet?! Is he for real? She turned her head to face him; to call him on his flattery, but he beat her to it.

"Don't worry about the Latin," he said. "I've told you we don't typically use it, and nobody I fish with uses it. It's just not important to the sport. The "bugs" thing is easy enough to get a handle on; there are only a few species of flying insects that are important to know in Maine and only a handful of underwater insects to learn. And of course there are the baitfish and leeches. All that stuff is good to learn during the winter months."

Annie listened patiently and started to realize she was going to have to stay patient when Chris started talking fly fishing. She wanted to know all this, but also wanted to simply *be* with him.

"Why don't we just work on the casting for today," he said, "and if you have any time tomorrow we'll go over the insect world as it relates to fly fishing. At least a bit of it."

Annie didn't respond, other than a smile. Chris looked at her differently now. He realized he'd been going on for some time about the sport, and that his passion for one thing was arresting his passion for something else. He tried to adopt a more lackadaisical affect. "What do you think so far?" he asked.

"I think I understand...I think I get it," she said, and then thought to herself, *And I think you'd better kiss me soon.*

Chris was staring at her now, enthralled by how her blonde hair seemed to absorb the late morning sun, and how just above her temples, where her hairline was permanently swept back, her hair was slightly lighter there; it was not golden, it was not white, and it was not yellow. He was sure it was a color he had not seen anywhere else in nature.

Chris wanted to treat Annie with the respect she deserved, but by God, he wanted her more than he had ever wanted anyone before. Should he kiss her? Should he hold her...or keep some distance? It was agonizing. What did she want from him? His desire to be with her was far beyond sex. He wanted to share everything with her. He wanted to travel with her, and learn with her...and learn *about* her. There was so much he didn't know yet. Did she like to try new foods? Did she snore? Did she like sex? Had she *had* sex? What kind of music did she like, the Blues, or classical, or God forbid, that new pop music they call "Country," or did she prefer Bob Wills, Patsy Cline and Faron Young? Or did she like all music. For all he knew, she was a head-banger, but he doubted it.

If he kissed her now (it would be a deep, meaningful, three minute, make you sweat, and maybe even curl your toes, kind of kiss) would she recoil? Would it put her off? If he pushed too quickly, he ran the risk of reducing any esteem he might hold in her eyes. Annie sure seemed to be the kind of woman who needed to take things slowly. Of this he was certain, and while he was pondering this, Annie placed the palm of her hand on his right cheek and gently turned his face towards hers. She leaned into him, carefully, and looked straight into his eyes. She searched them, looking farther into them, past the blue-grey pupils, trying to find some assurance, reciprocity...even safety. And she found all those things in the chambers of his loving eyes, and as she did, Chris found the calm permission he sought and he felt a gravity he'd never experienced before.

Both of them kept their eyes open and as their lips met. Chris felt a warmth and a glow, and a joy so foreign to him he became emotional. It seemed to him to be the noblest emotion he'd ever felt, one of expanding love. This was no longer flirting...it was love. He looked at her face – her beautiful face – and she seemed almost in a trance, but smiling. He felt dismay, as well as love, as a hundred thoughts raced through his mind. There were obstacles in their way...his lifestyle and hers; he had to finish school, her dedication to her father and to the farm, and the objections he anticipated from his well-to-do father. But as fast as these thoughts raced in, Chris pushed them out, for he was already committed to Annie.

Annie seemed as if she was in a trance, as she felt the strength of his love envelop her. Her lips were passive no longer, and she kissed him fully and hard. She held him tighter, and felt her excitement growing when Chris turned his head. They saw Tom walking up the bank. When he reached them they were both on their feet.

"Any luck?" asked Chris.

"Two small ones. Did you see the stones coming off?"

"No," said Chris. "We've been learning to cast. Were they the big stoneflies, or those little yellow ones?" Tom held up his thumb and index finger less than an inch apart. At that point Chris watched the sunlit opening above the brook where the branches of the alders and maples parted. There were a few insects flittering about, but he didn't see any stoneflies with their tell-tale double wings laboring towards the foliage on the stream banks.

"I'm going to keep working upstream," said Tom, and he gave a smiling wave as he walked off. Chris started wondering if Tom wasn't feeling left out, with all his attention focused on Annie. His friend was a big boy, and had given his blessing—but still. Annie just said, "He's a great guy, we should do something for him."

"Well," said Chris, "He loves to eat, and his favorite meal is chicken tikka masala."

Annie nodded her head. "I'll ask Benny for the recipe."

That same evening, the house was empty except for Chris and Annie. Tom was out with Annie's father, learning how to drive the old Ford 8N tractor. He was having the time of his life. There was little chance they would be coming in soon.

Annie was busy with her cooking tasks. While she cooked, she thought about where their newfound love would lead them. As she ground the cumin seeds, she contemplated the barriers ahead. She heard Chris come down the old creaking stairs from his shower and he came into the kitchen and leaned against the doorway. He was dressed in some well-worn Levi's, and a salmon-colored, canvas button-up shirt. He looked beautiful, she thought. There was still a lingering doubt that a life together was a remote possibility. She wanted dearly to let this hour endure, and she moved to him. Earlier on the stream all he talked about was fly casting, but now he extended both arms inviting her.

There was a slight hesitation on her part, but only for a moment. He held her tight against his chest, drawing her into him, speechlessly, meaningfully. Then he spoke in a whisper, "I fell in love with you this week. I can't explain it, but I want to be honest. I never expected this...hell, I didn't even *want* this." He paused for a moment. "I know it's crazy...and I don't expect you to feel the same, I just want you to know. We're leaving in a couple of days."

Annie looked lovingly at him. "Yes, I feel it too...but I don't want to talk about it."

"But Annie! Why not talk about it?"

"Because if we do discuss it, I would have to be...sensible, and I'd rather not just now. It's been wonderful, and I feel deep down that it can't last."

"Why? Why can't it last? Why can't it last for our lifetimes?" But he also worried about the difficulties of any arrangement that might allow them to stay together.

She wiped her hands with a towel. "I'll just say it! My home – my life – is so different from yours." It was the only way she knew to put it. "I don't have an education, although I might have, and all I am is a farm girl. You're an international traveler, a mountain climber...you speak Italian, for God's sake! And Chris, what would your parents think?"

"They would love you." He hugged her again and kissed her cheek. "Dad would adore you."

"What about your mother? It scares me that you left her out."

"Oh, she would also...it's just that I've never talked about women to her. Maybe a little...but I don't really know how she feels. You must realize, Annie, that it's not just your beauty. Everything you say and do makes me understand how good and wonderful you are. Those same qualities will endear you to them."

"But that's the thing. I'm not good, and I can be selfish. What can you have learned of me in four days? And in two more days you'll be gone."

"I'll be coming back in September, thank God." He had a serious, resigned look on his face. "And Annie, I knew everything I needed to know about you the day I met you. The first time you spoke. The first time I looked into your eyes."

"In five months! Anything can happen in that time. A hundred things that can make a spring love affair a distant memory." She buried her face in his chest, and then looked up at him. "Kiss me, Chris, whatever happens; let me feel like this for a while longer."

She shut her eyes and he kissed her again, and again, and again. And the hour did endure.

ELEVEN

There were two more mornings of fishing, and Annie got better with every cast. On the second day of lessons she caught her first fish on a fly, a seven-inch brookie on a cream-colored Stimulator. The two hiked a mile up Lewis Brook and found a pretty little plunge pool just below the deadwater that stretched for another half-mile upstream. Through the heavy cedar boughs they could see the light from the openness at the deadwater, and the black, flat, water. Directly in front of them in the darkness of the forest, the impacted water shot between two huge boulders, and dropped about a foot into the pool where it churned up some white foam and bubbles.

Chris and Annie snuck up on the tail of the pool, a good forty feet from the boulders and surveyed the water. The current fell into the pool, playing off the shape of the big rocks, and the ripples and the bubbles followed the length of the pool along the right-hand side, and slowed again where they stood. It was a beautiful place. The cedars overhung the banks which were everywhere covered in a thick, spongy moss. The sunlight peeked through the dark branches where it could, making even the mid-day sun seem like the warm light of the late afternoon. In some spots, there were ferns two feet high, starting to uncurl and stretch out for the summer. "I've lived down the road my whole life, and I didn't know this place was here," she said. "It's perfect."

Chris whispered, "Do you see that film of bubbles riding along the current?" He pointed his rod tip towards the row of foam and ripples. "That's your feeding lane – well, the inner edge of it, actually. The trout will lie under there in the nice, cool oxygenated water and wait for anything edible to come floating downstream. They're pretty opportunistic. Depending on who you talk to, around ninety percent of what they eat is underwater, so they watch for nymphs of different insects, or pupae. Sometimes they're lucky enough to find leeches, and once they get big enough, the brookies will go after smaller fish. At the right time of year, fish start looking up for the adult versions of those nymphs and pupae of the caddis flies, or of the mayflies like the ones we saw downstream earlier. Later in the summer, there will be lots of bugs like grasshoppers, beetles and spiders floating down from the deadwater where it meanders through the meadow. While trout like leeches, they *love* grasshoppers. This is perfect! I'll give you some Joe's Hoppers. Tell me you'll come back here in July and fish this spot again."

"I'll try," she replied, and thought, *I don't even have a fly rod.*

One of the boulders near the tail of the pool was rather flat, and tapered down into the water's edge, and most of it was hidden behind a short, squat cedar whose trunk swept towards the water and then bolted skyward. The fisheye view from the pool would be obstructed. Chris positioned Annie on one knee behind the cedar. She thought the soft moss made a nice cushion as she readied herself to make the first cast to the head of the pool. She flicked the rod tip gently until ten or twelve feet of fly line was laying on the rock at her feet. She eyed the head of the pool, and spied the spot she wanted to drift the fly just along the sudsy feeding lane inside the far bank. She patiently checked the trees behind her to see if there was enough room for a back cast, but it was a tangled mess of branches. "You'll have to cast side-arm, along the surface of the water," whispered Chris. Annie had already figured it out. She was thinking like an angler. She drew her rod tip straight skyward, and cast it forward with authority just as Chris had shown her, and executed a perfect roll cast to get the line airborne. But before the fly could hit the water she started the sidearm back cast and followed with several false casts, all the while paying out more line. When she felt she had enough line to reach the white suds, she ended the forward cast with a slight, downward pressure with her right thumb. The line responded, and the tight little loop at its end unfurled, softly delivering the fly about three feet above where she felt the trout were holding. She was proud of her cast, and Chris was certain she didn't even realize how perfect it actually was. Before she could make any kind of adjustment with her tackle, there was a vicious strike at the fly. Annie gasped and quickly snapped the rod tip up. The fly line, the leader, the tippet and the fly flew backwards and landed in a tangled ball in front of her at the base of the rock.

Chris chuckled. "Man! He really wanted that!"

"What'd I do wrong, besides almost strangling myself with the line?" asked Annie.

"Well, rather than raising the rod tip to set the hook, you can just leave the tip down parallel to the water and make a quick, but gentle, strip of the line with your left hand. That way, if you miss the fish, the fly will only scoot forward, but stays on the water. The fish may think the bug's trying to get away. Not only might the trout keep after it and hit it again, but the line will be in a position that you will be able to pick it up and make another cast, instead of in a pile at your feet."

"Sorry", said Annie.

"Oh God, don't be sorry! Actually you're doing better than most. Most people at this point are still trying to cast like it's a spinning rod. Let's try again. If we didn't scare him and put him down, he'll try for it again."

Annie was still in position to cast. She made sure her fly line wasn't tangled on the rock, and that she wasn't kneeling on it. She wanted that fish. And Chris wanted it for her. But while he was admiring her perfect blonde ponytail, Annie was all business.

He's still there, she said to herself.

God, she smells great! he thought.

Keep the rhythm of the cast... don't slap the water with the fly...

Chris: *I wonder if she really thinks she loves me.*

Throughout the ages that people have fly fished, anglers young and old have fallen in love with the sport. When it takes, it takes like hell, and there follows a lifelong love and affection. Sometimes, it's rather more like an affliction. Annie was falling in love, with Chris, for sure, but also with the art of fly fishing. She was subconsciously allowing this "affliction" into her life, embracing the notion that here was an activity which she felt great about, one which she could do for year after year, in complete peace, with a modicum of skill. She felt high as a kite. *Why didn't I try this before, when she watched Ben all those times, casting and catching salmon and then releasing them?* she thought.

While she was sorting through this new, profound wonder, Chris was watching her cast, wondering what Annie looked like naked. His thoughts made him feel pathetic because he knew her mind was elsewhere, but he couldn't control it, he was crazy about this girl, and he was excited.

Annie pulled the line through the stripping guide, and started her back cast. With only two false casts, she let the fly land on the water, just outside of the sudsy line in the current. Almost as soon as the fly hit the water, there was a flash as the trout hit again. Annie was a good student. She instinctively wanted to raise the rod tip again, but didn't. She stripped the line quickly about eight inches, but she had a little slack in the line where it was caught in the current and she missed the hookset. But Chris was right; the eight-inch strip only took up the slack and moved the fly a few inches downstream. In the time it took Annie to realize she was doing everything correctly, the fish tried to eat it again. This time there was no slack in the fly line. This time she stripped quickly, and the line tightened and the hook struck home. She had him. Chris yelled, "That's it!"

Annie felt the tug and slowly lifted the rod tip. While she never took her eyes off the thrashing trout, she could see the bend in the three-weight rod in her peripheral vision. She was surprised at how strong the fish was in such a little brook.

"Just keep stripping ever so slowly," said Chris, his hand lightly touching her shoulder. She did, stripping with her left hand where the line was cradled between her right index finger and the butt of the rod. "Try to bring him to the left, into this slack water," he said. "Easy does it."

Chris dipped his net into the water where the rock jutted into the brook. "He's tired now," said Chris. "Ease him to me." Up came the shallow net with the brookie lying in it. He held it out for her to see. It was beautiful—a plump little trout, dark and pretty, with the small yellowish-white Stimulator still in the corner of its mouth. The fly complemented perfectly the red and yellow and blue spots on its side, set off by the white leading edges of the trout's fins. After only a moment Chris took the barbless hook out of the fish's jaw. He slid it back into the water where it swam slowly away, seeming more annoyed than hurt. Annie shook her head twice, smiling at the little pool in amazement and then swung around and hugged Chris with her left arm. He smiled back, and they kissed under the cedar branches with the dappled sunlight highlighting their faces.

"Sit for a while before we head back," said Chris.

They sat farther up on the bank on a flat mossy spot, and Chris took her in his arms and drew her down, lying next to him. This place is perfect, Annie thought, with the emerald moss, and filtered sunlight and the gentle babble of the brook. This was *their* spot now, she thought. They kissed again, a long unwavering kiss. Chris was committed now. He could be true to Annie like no other. That was something he was fully capable of. He knew it, and Annie knew it.

"Annie...," he whispered. His desire mounting, his hand on her bare leg advanced to her thigh and he pushed himself up as if he would lie upon her. She was afraid of *everything* at that moment, and she trembled slightly beneath his touch. She did not move. It was he who said suddenly aloud, "No," and removed his hand. They lay there for a while, only kissing. Annie's world fell away, and now there was only the weight of his perfect body upon her. She held his hips close against hers.

******

The lights of Roslyn had gone out one by one. In the early morning hours the farmhouse was quiet. Even the new stray barn cat Chris had named "K2" was too tired to hunt for the mice and voles. But there were two who could not sleep, one of whom could only think of that mossy rock, and the perpetual murmuring of the brook. An intermittent, unyielding temptation lay with Chris. In only a few hours he and Tom would leave Annie and the farm. His mind remained fixed on that time by the brook when he moved to make love to her, and though she had trembled, Annie had made no move to stop him. He felt she would have given herself to him. Chris wanted their relationship to be different from any she had had with other men. He was certain, in fact, that an absolute tenderness and respect would see her at the altar. He hoped it would. There would be conflicts and dozens of social difficulties before them—or was he imagining it? It's not the nineteenth century, for God's sake! He thought of going to her, of innocently holding her once more before he left—innocently, as on the mossy bank.

Annie left her light on. She was a farm girl, and though she was a virgin, she knew how things worked. If he wanted her, he could have it all, though it still caused the same fear and anxiety a girl in 1895 might have. The fact was, her desire was more for his pleasure than for hers.

She lay there waiting, breathing, imagining. He didn't come. He was worrying more for her comfort than for his own desires. Exhausted, they both finally fell asleep, with lights burning.

Morning was breaking throughout the valley, tumbling down the mountainsides with all its matter-of-factness, while Annie was fixing an early breakfast. She was working as fast as she could as the jeep was backed up on the lawn close to the kitchen porch. Tom and Chris were piling bags into it as Mr. Nielson came in from the barn to see their guests off.

"Well, boys," John said, "I'm real sorry ta see ya goin'. I didn't want to take in guests, but I've actually enjoyed it." John looked at his daughter with a forlorn smile. "And so has Annie, I think. She tells me you might be comin' back in the fall."

"I definitely am. Tom's not sure if he can make it," replied Chris.

There was a pause for a moment before John said, "Okay, drive safe boys...say ya goodbye's, Annie," and headed back to the barn.

Chris slid into the driver's seat, and Annie, instead of giving him a kiss or saying goodbye, shut the jeep's door, as if it was no big deal.

Tom said, "It's been wonderful, Annie. I really enjoyed it. And don't stop fishing."

And Chris said, "Three weeks next time. I'll come the first of September. And I'll write."

A resigned, sad nod of the head was her only response, and with a wink from Chris the jeep sped down the road towards Interstate 95. Annie walked slowly into the house to change her clothes, and as she did something caught her eye in the kitchen doorway. It was a fly rod in its tube, a vest, a net, some fly boxes and a reel with extra spools. The vest was draped over the rod tube and there was a note pinned to it with the inscription *Annie Darlin'*.

******

The entire summer to pass by. May was rainier than usual, and John and Annie had to put in two extra plantings of squash and cucumbers, which took root eventually. By early June, the planting was all done. Annie did fish, often and would sometimes go back to "The Pool" up Lewis Brook to try her luck. She caught a few small trout, but none as nice as her first. She would always start with a Stimulator, but would try other flies if that didn't work. Sometimes she just sat in the moss by the flat rock at the tail of The Pool, and daydreamed about her time there with Chris, when they almost made love. She would bring his letters with her, when she got them. Her mind was far away, first in Boston, and then Europe. She imagined herself on trips with Chris, backpacking through Scotland with their fly rods in aluminum tubes strapped to the outside of their packs, and the click of their telescoping walking sticks on the old country roads. She dreamed of it all. She wanted it all. She dreamed euphoric agonies of love, amongst the fields and streams and the slow ebb and flow of Roslyn.

In July, there was a shortage of guests in Roslyn. There were very few at the Nielson's farm. John had seen a *Rick Steve's Europe* episode on Maine Public Television, where there were some farmers in Italy or Spain (he couldn't remember which) who rented rooms to travelers and incorporated farming into the experience. It worked for the farmers and the tourists seemed to love it. So the Nielson Farm became Roslyn's first agriturismo, although when John made up some leaflets he spelled it *Agritouristimo*. When they did have guests, Annie was her normal, cheerful self, going about all her chores. For the most part, Annie kept to herself as far as the sports were concerned. In those full summer days, she would sometimes go to bed as soon as it became dark, and lying there in her half-sleep her mind would quickly be back at The Pool, or lying in the grass by the brook were Chris gave her that first casting lesson. She longed for those moments that seemed now like years ago! She would lie there going over the memorized lines from his letters: "adore...All my love...long to kiss you." *How serious was he?*

And she questioned herself in the most solemn way; was she ready for September? On some nights, even when she was dead tired from the farm work, she would lie in her bed, raging. Not in anger, but her emotions exploded in the dark. One warm, humid, August night, she imagined Chris was with her; she softly brushed her hair behind one ear. She could not feel the warmth of his kiss on her lips, but she felt him lay his hand flat on her belly, and move it slowly to her side and slide his fingers down to her bare hip bone. It moved up her side – tickling a little – and the palm of his hand cupped the side of her breast, his thumb sliding across her nipple. Only for a second, as if he was teasing her. Her breathing now was as if she was starved for oxygen, her lungs taking a full measure of air with every breath. Before she knew what was happening his hand was on her thigh, *high* on her thigh, moving closer, and closer, and closer. She began to sweat. He quickly found exactly where to touch, and how to touch and how to move, and there in the dark there was another explosion. This wasn't her first time by any means, but Annie knew then, lying alone in her bed once she caught her breath, that September couldn't arrive fast enough, and it was in exhausted happiness that she fell asleep.

That summer her friendship with Doc Warren ripened. She found she could tell him (and only him) some of her deepest thoughts. One morning as she walked to the river wearing her fly vest and with her rod in hand, she stopped to talk with Arno and Ennis who were in their own gear, heading in the opposite direction on their way to Lewis Brook. It was a quick chat, and ended with Annie asking Doc if he would mind stopping by that evening for a few moments.

"Of course, my dear," he said, smiling. "We can chat about anything you like."

That evening they sat together on the kitchen porch, Arno in a big wicker chair and his feet up on a foot stool. "Now, Annie, let's have it."

She began with explaining her sadness about being on the farm so much that she seldom spent any time around any really well-educated people, and it was difficult to find any informative books because the library in Millinocket was too far away. The internet was available some places, but like many people she preferred books, by far. She'd be twenty next month. Time, she told the doctor, was passing her by.

Arno laughed aloud at that. "My Lord, you're right! We certainly must do something quick, before it's too late. What would you like to read, my dear?"

"Browning, maybe, and Shakespeare...I read *Othello* last year...it was a great play."

"I can lend you some books, but you know Annie, there are many educated people right here in Roslyn. Find some of them to talk to."

"I couldn't...I'd feel...funny."

"What about Ben Garrison? He's a scholar for certain."

"*Benny?* A scholar? But he only went to high school."

"He's read all of my books, all of Ennis's, and the only thing he spends his money on besides good food and wine is books, books and more books."

"He usually has a book with him, now that you mention it," she said. "But he's so shy. Do you think he'll have a serious conversation with me?"

"Not about himself, certainly, but he'd talk to you about any of his books or about almost any topic."

Doc hesitated as though he didn't want to speak out-of-school. "You know, Annie, he's quite learned about many things...there are just certain parts of life that have eluded him. It'd be good for him, as well. He's the one you want, I'm sure of it."

And so the friendship between Annie and Ben Garrison blossomed that summer. When they met at the post office or on the street, instead of a cordial greeting, they stood and talked for a while about Dickens, or Twain, or whatever book Ben had most recently loaned her. The second book she returned to him was the *Essays of E.B. White.* They sat for hours in the study in his cabin, discussing the many topics White wrote about, and how Ben thought he was the best American essayist in the last hundred years. Ben was genuinely interested in everything Annie had to say about the books she read, and the two spent many happy evenings there as the summer went on.

In July, when the guest list at the farm lightened, Annie fished more and more. Early one cool morning as she rode her bicycle to Ben's cottage to borrow a book he recommended about fly fishing, she saw him swing his old Bronco into the yard across from Doc Warren's office. She wore her fly vest, and her rod, in its tube, was strapped across her handlebars. Ben's "town house" was coming along nicely. The golden peeled logs looked warm and straight in the sharp morning sunlight. There were no cedar—all the logs were either spruce or fir. Ben had peeled the logs right there in the yard by hand using a peeling spud and draw knives, and the lines and markings from the knives only made the logs more charming. He had no tractor. Each log was rolled up on purlins to form the next course in the wall, using a simple rope and a pulley anchored to the opposite wall, and he moved each log with no help.

The cabin's four walls were nearly finished. All four plate logs were in position to be rolled up the purlins to each top. Once that was accomplished, he would place the rafters and then build the roof. There were more windows than is traditionally used in log homes, which were framed out, as were both the doorways. The plywood subfloor was swept clean of shavings and sawdust.

Ben was already out of the Ford and inside the roofless four walls when Annie coasted into the driveway.

"Hello, the house!" she called out. Ben stepped into the doorway, smiling.

"Good morning, Annie. Where're you headed?"

"Thought I'd hike up Lewis to the deadwater...see if I can scare up some trout with hoppers."

"Nice." he said. "Try orange, this time of year."

Annie knew nothing of Ben's imprisoned love, nor the pain *and* the pleasure that their new close association gave him. Nobody knew. Ben made certain these matters stayed unnoticed.

Ben was the best gardener in the valley, everybody knew that, and was probably a better grower that John Nielson. But Ben didn't grow vegetables for sale, just seedlings, so as not to compete directly with his neighbor. John never grew garlic because Ben was so good at it. If anyone needed garlic, they either went to Ben's cabin or mentioned it to him when they saw him. Ben grew a lot of good, strong garlic. With only himself to take care of, he could live as frugally as he wanted. Nobody in town knew it, but three years earlier Ben had saved enough money to take a trip to Europe and tour the French countryside. While he was there he found in an open market a strain of Russian Red garlic that he loved. He bought some seed stock, shipped it home and after a couple of seasons he had quite a crop. He had grown other domestic varieties for years, experimenting with growing techniques for such a northern climate, and had perfected them.

She asked for a book recommendation. He suggested a couple and told her she could come by the cabin to pick some out. He would cook supper.

When Annie arrived at the cottage, she returned *Flowers for Algernon*. Ben had prepared the meal for them. It was a warm evening, and he made a nice garden salad with a homemade vinaigrette dressing. He had earlier made a garlic scape and potato soup, and served it with coq au vin and a nice 2004 Cabernet Franc Reserve. The time spent together was an education for them both. They talked for hours and the conversation and wine flowed freely. They reviewed Keyes' *Flowers*, a short story that touches upon several moral and ethical themes. One topic is the treatment of the mentally challenged. Annie had gained so much respect for Ben by this time that it never occurred to her there might be a correlation between any of the topics in the book and his own experiences (if only in a small way). His issue was physical. People had often pre-judged him because of his gait and appearance. Now, in Annie's eyes Ben could do anything, and more importantly, he could do anything extremely *well*.

She asked about the garlic scapes. He explained that the scapes are the long, leafless flowering stem that rises directly from the bulb. "Soon after they appear they will begin to curl into a loop-de-loop. When they do, you snap them off before they flower. Breaking them off encourages the plant to put more energy into bulb production," he explained. "They're a delicacy in some cultures. I have some pretty extensive notes about growing garlic, if you or your dad would like to borrow them."

Ben walked Annie home late that night, and when they parted Annie asked if she could come by the next Saturday to peruse his bookcases. On the way home, Ben several times had to stop himself from dreaming of a different life...the one with Annie. *Stay the course*, he would say to himself.

In all their pleasant evenings together Annie had not talked about Chris other than to mention that he was coming back in September. By now the wagging tongues around town had all gossiped about the two love birds. Ben tried to not pay attention to any of it, but still he had overheard some of it—*half engaged, engaged,* and *love-struck*. He accepted it, but it was hard to bear. Saturday morning Ben phoned Annie from The Riverdriver and asked her if she'd like to stay for supper. It was nearly September, and Ben wanted at least one more evening with her before she became indisposed.

When she arrived, the cabin smelled wonderful. He had been cooking for some time. Being cooler outside, there was a golden glow in the fieldstone fireplace.

Small amber flames danced on the handsome log walls. Annie was dressed in a soft beige sweater and blue jeans, her hair in a simple French braid. She was lovely. When she came into the living room and saw the flowers, the wineglasses, and the attractive patterned plates, she gasped. "Ben, you've gone to all this trouble! You really are something, you know. No one's ever gone to this much trouble for me."

Ben looked at her with his handsome eyes as if to say, "You're worth it," but instead said with a smile, "I enjoy it. Supper will be ready in about twenty minutes, why don't you pick out your book while I finish?" He handed her a glass of Alsace Riesling.

Annie went into the study next to the dining area and looked through the cases. She had looked many times before, but just now was noticing the section of Arctic exploration, and the vast collection of field guides. There were three whole shelves dedicated to fly fishing.

"Do you have any recommendations?" she called into the kitchen.

"I've been thinking of Dickens, or maybe some of Isak Dinesen's stories," he called back.

Annie continued looking around the room. "I love this wine!" she said. But he didn't reply. There was a door that was ajar in the back corner of the study which led to a small room. As she walked by she could see more books in it, and she tentatively pushed the door all the way open. It was a store room. A big walk-in closet, actually, and Annie stepped into it just a foot or two. There was enough moonlight shining through a window for her to see, and she was stunned. The entire room was packed with literature, boxes and boxes of books. There must have been several thousand pieces. Not just books, but periodicals—more boxes of them. And there were maps, and pamphlets, and several sets of encyclopedias. There were old books, and new books still in wrappers, and a Bible, the Quran, and the Torah. There were audiobooks and dictionaries. There was a very large framed sign leaning against the back wall of the room. It was more than seven feet long and three feet wide and she could see there was nothing written on it. The light was poor that far in the room, but she noticed the intricately carved scrollwork on the wide frame. It was simple and elegant. It looked unfinished, and she thought, is there anything this guy can't do? She backed out into the study and put the door as it was.

When she went back to the dining area Ben said, "Voila!" They sat down to the meal and, as usual, it was nothing short of spectacular:

Scallops Poullet
Cornish Game Hens with Garlic and Rosemary
Pommes Frites
Sautéed Asparagus

And a second bottle of Riesling. They laughed and talked, and it occurred to Annie it was the first time she had heard Ben laugh out loud. It was nice.

While they shared the meal together (Annie, at times speechless with admiration), they talked of a hundred things, and listened to Van Morrison's *Moondance* CD from the next room. It was only after they were seated in front of the fire with their wineglasses when their conversation turned to more serious topics. Both stared at the fire for a moment before speaking. They had different things on their minds, but both felt an unfamiliar comfort and ease.

Annie spoke first, as usual. "Ben, could I ask you two sort of heavy questions?"

"Well," said Ben, "I have one for you, so we can take turns."

Annie was finishing a sip of her wine, "No," she said, smiling, "These past months you've cooked for me, helped me, and listened to me, and I've done all the talking. I've done nothing for you. You go first...I insist."

Ben took a drink and winced a little. "All right." He looked her in the eye. "It's personal. But first I want to say you've done more for me than you could possibly know." Annie stiffened a little. She had no idea what he wanted to know. "Fire away," she said.

Ben paused as if he wanted to back-track, and then asked, "Are you engaged to Mr. Phelps?"

"Call him Chris, please Ben, he would want you to. The short answer is no. I love him...I'm sure I do. And he has professed his love for me...but we've made no commitments, and we've spent time together for only two weeks. It was very intense, though, at least for me."

Ben reclined into his corner of the sofa, listening intently. He looked scholarly and attractive. His back and neck deformity were invisible now, and since he was sitting, his slightly strange limp was nonexistent. He looked more distinguished than old Doc Warren. He was tracing his finger along the rim of his wineglass, and said nothing.

"There are some socio-economic issues," she said, staring at the fire. "But he's really a down-to-earth person, Ben, and I know we both want the same things in life, it's just going to be...difficult."

"And there's the farm, and your father," said Ben.

"And there's the farm," she replied, nodding her head in a sort of resignation. "You know, Ben, Chris is quite intrigued by you." Ben looked away from her quickly. He was most uncomfortable with the notion of anyone paying attention to him at all, even noticing him. "He thinks you're an amazing guy. And so do I." He stared at his glass, feeling cornered. "I'd like to know your thoughts about it."

Ben shifted his weight on the sofa. "I don't know Chris at all, but I do think you shouldn't worry one bit about anything socio-economic, and as far as your father is concerned, I know he will just want you to be happy. The farm and everything else will work itself out."

"It's hard not to worry."

"But you must try," he said, "You're both smart, industrious people. You'll make enough money and do well. And social stratigraphy is absolutely meaningless. Worrying about one's station in society – or where one fits in it – is a colossal waste of time. You marry for love...nothing else."

"We'll see. He's arriving in a couple of weeks. I'm not as excited as I thought I'd be. I think because I dwelt on his return so much, so intensely over the summer, I exhausted myself."

Ben smiled. He was smiling a lot. "It's the passage of time," he said. "As time goes by, everything changes. Don't worry, it'll be wonderful."

Then he said, "Question one."

"Okay," she said, "I'm afraid I've been snooping. The door to your store room was open, and I took the liberty of looking." Ben looked at her as if he was waiting for an actual question.

"Ben...that's a lot of literature, what are you doing with all that? Have you *read* it all?"

"It certainly is a lot. I'd love to get it all out of there. It's nothing, really. It started as a project when I was sixteen years old and the collecting hasn't completely stopped. And yes, I suppose I've read a great deal of it. Still picking away at it."

It wasn't much of an answer, but she couldn't come up with a follow-up question that might make him divulge more without pressing him too much.

"Question number two," she said. "In that room you had the Quran, the Bible and the Torah, but I haven't seen one religious artifact in your beautiful house. It's interesting, is all. You might be the most spiritual person I've ever met. I was just wondering...do you subscribe to any one religion?"

Ben sat up a little and poured himself some more wine, and then filled Annie's glass. "Wouldn't you like to ask something easier, like, what's the meaning of life?"

"I'm sorry; it's just that, you just seem to be so...comfortable. So much at peace with yourself and with life. I'm not looking for any secrets or anything, I'm just interested."

"Good, because I don't think I have any secrets—or answers. I may have found a formula for life that works for me. You know, because of my orthopaedic problems, I haven't always been...involved in mainstream society. By keeping to myself for all these years I have had time for learning and introspection." He paused for a moment to collect his thoughts. He had never talked to anyone in the community before about his problems, except to Doc about his physical issues, and now he was telling Annie everything, and sounding a little like a monk. But now he was all in.

He continued to wax philosophical. He told her he believed that people belonged to two different orders of existence. One is their time-based existence in the world they know, the other an eternal existence, as a place not in history, but in nature. He believed – or hoped – that the second order was more like a dimension, one based in knowledge and acceptance. The body is just a vessel which must deteriorate and die, but if one truly accepted the second order, one would know a kind of inner happiness. He looked at Annie. She was staring at him, blinking.

She didn't understand at all what he was saying, but that wasn't her fault. He was completely unprepared to verbalize such things. "Ben," she said, "I love that you have such faith." All he heard was, "*I love* blah *you* blah blah."

"I don't think of it as simply faith, but also a trust," he replied. But she was here, and she was listening, and she was interested, so he went on to tell her about his interpretation of God. God in his eyes was light, and love and most of all, the gift of life. He found his evidence not in church, but in the "mountains, and the streams and in the plants in the ground." He was making a little more sense now, and it was lovely. But she wanted more.

"Do you think I'm silly," he asked, "that streams and flowers and the forests teach me the same things about God as intellectual or deeply spiritual people do?"

"Silly?" she replied. "I think you're beautiful." He nearly fell over. He knew she meant something different, but it sounded wonderful. They were in deep now, and he kept going. He told her that in his solitude these past twenty four years, he had found not only beauty in nature, but also profundity *and* simplicity...and answers; answers to his own questions, whether he asked them or not. "God chooses to channel His beauty through nature," he said, and then looked from her eyes to the crackling fire, "and through some people."

"I was raised Christian. You know that, Annie." She nodded. "And I know your faith is important to you, so I don't want this to sound too weird for you." There was a pause while Ben collected his thoughts, and then almost giggled as he said, "You mentioned my faith, and I get how ironic this sounds, but my faith sort of *evolved*. I have kept to myself for so long, that much of my personal communion has always been in nature," he looked at the fire, "and in reflection.

"For Christians," he said, "Communion is supposed to be practiced over and over throughout their life, in remembrance of Him...to give thanks for all He did for us. And I have always embraced that. But some of my fellow Christians feel their goal in life is "to be with God" and to do this they must rise above Earth and escape from such an imperfect world. For me, there isn't much in nature that isn't perfect. Only people are imperfect." Ben glanced at her sideways. "Present company excepted."

"Oh, I'm a long way from perfect," she replied.

"Well...you might not be perfect." His eyes smiled. "But you're perfect enough."

Ben told her how when he stands alone in a river, or walks along the mountain trails, he often feels the Universal Being flow through him. He couldn't explain it in any details, just that this communion with nature gave him a kind of central peace. He was pretty vague, but Annie's heart leaped to his every word. The soft, golden light from the propane lamp flickered off his perfect, straight and angular face and it gave him a serene affect. In the emotional turmoil of her young, absent love, and the very thought of abandoning her father to work the farm alone, she had longed recently to feel the lightness of God's love, and for some guidance, and was amazed to find that while she had always gone to Mass fairly regularly, Ben's explanations of his own beliefs made her feel more...alive.

Ben, more in love than ever, was in a happy place for he knew he had connected with Annie. He suspected that it was a friendship unlike any other for her, and he was right. Annie felt something for Ben also—a deep, personal link, and an admiration for the spirit he had become. Here was a crippled man who had accepted his afflictions, embraced the essence of life itself and made the most of his short time on earth with a grace so beautiful it defied account. The simplest flowers and insects suggested to him the meaning of his life. And although he had had many philosophical discussions with Doc over the years (one of their favorite pastimes), Ben had shared his deepest feelings – all but one – with Annie. She knew it and it made her glow.

TWELVE

The black jeep sped up the grade where the road entered the south end of Roslyn. Chris sat alone in the seat and instead of the teasing and kidding when Tom was with him in the springtime, he had only apprehension as his companion, and he was driving like the proverbial bat out of hell in an effort to rid himself of the feeling he was experiencing. It was a feeling of melancholy he sometimes had when he was alone and introspective. During the summer, he had worked some, and had made a pilgrimage to a few of the storied salmon rivers of Scotland, and had been skunked. Every waking minute he had longed for Annie, and every sleeping moment he dreamed of her, of a future with her in a permanent union. He had written her, often, but he couldn't help but succumb to the fear that she might have changed her mind about him during the summer—whatever her mind was. She seemed distant at the moment he left with Tom last April, and he had supposed it was her way of dealing with the goodbye. She couldn't respond to his letters overseas and she had no internet service. The two letters he received upon arriving home were lovely and encouraging, but he *had* to see her.

Chris's father had piloted him towards a career in business for all his time, and although the young man had a scientific mind, his father knew it was industry (specifically Wall Street) that drove the world. Would Annie accept the fact that he was not religious? He had noticed the Catholic symbols and the crucifixes in most of the rooms in the farmhouse, or was it her late mother who had put them everywhere? He hated to think of such things; they only reminded him of the many obstacles in their way. He felt he would be able to contribute enough to be sure she would be comfortable; hell, he had a trust fund. And he knew he held the certain things that should be important to her, or to anyone: courage, compassion, friendliness, character. He had meant only to flirt with Annie but she had lit a flame in him. Now she was all he really wanted.

Annie did not see the jeep coming, though she had been watching for it from the window over the kitchen sink. It was when she returned from straightening the flowers and the cushions next to Chris's overstuffed chair that she saw it, already in the dooryard, with Chris already unpacking. Swinging open the old screen door, she saw Chris crossing the lawn, his bulging Lowe backpack slung over one shoulder, and his smaller daypack in which he kept his books, headlamp and shaving kit in his other hand. When he saw her, he laid the packs on the grass and spread his arms wide, and she fell into them. "Annie darlin'," he said with a sigh of relief.

"You've arrived." She hated it when other people pointed out the obvious.

"Yup, and only one hour late," he said. "And it'll be four weeks, this time. Tom couldn't make it (picking up his bags). Any other guests in the house?"

"Not just yet."

"Great! I was worried I'd never get you alone for the whole month." She blushed at this, but it pierced her with joy. She evaded responding, but said, "We haven't had many guests, as you would expect in July and August, but we did have one couple from New York recently. I think we're getting the hang of this agritourism thing. Only a few people other than

Tom have shown any interest in the farming—just the salmon and the trout." Chris wanted to put his arms around her as they walked to the porch, but his arms were full. He noticed a new sign over the porch roof that said, *"Nielson Farm Guests Welcome."*

As they reached the porch, Chris laid his packs down, and when he turned to hug Annie again John Nielson spied them. "Well, hello! Good ta see ya again, son. Good to see him back, isn't it, Annie?"

"Yes...it is," she said, squinting at Chris in the afternoon sun.

She led Chris to his room, and as they went in she said, "This was Tom's, but it's a better room, with a nicer view of the fields."

He noticed more fresh cut flowers next to the bed. "It's lovely," was all he said. She was pretending to be professional – at least a little – and she reminded him where there were clean towels. He reached down, took her hand, and drew her to him. There was no invitation to kiss, just kissing, and lots of it. Suddenly, he held her face in both his hands. He looked at her beautiful smile, and her lovely eyes framed by her blonde hair with a single thin braid down one side, and said, "Annie I *do* love you, even more, if that's possible." He said it as if he was still shocked at the level of his conviction.

He spoke no word of marriage.

"And I love you, Chris. There's a lot we have to talk about, don't you think?" She was well aware of the difficulties before them. She broke from the long embrace and, with a devilish smile and a giggle said, "I have to start something for supper."

But as her hands prepared the lemon chicken, her thoughts were of the same old dilemma. *Chris does love me...and I know I love him...it's just so fast. But*

131

here he is. Father Michaud would probably think it wicked if I gave myself to him now...but it's love! It is giving, is it not? If I believe something to be right but it's different from the church's views, I can't help it. It's what I feel – it is truth, and I'm going to stay true to myself.

No matter what she told herself, she kept hearing a voice, "Annie, please don't do this...not yet." And she kept answering the voice, *Yes, and lose him, and be stuck here forever.*

So she resolved to find a way to satisfy both her passionate craving for a life of happiness, and the old desire to "be good." A resolution seemed attainable.

******

The four weeks that stretched before them offered a gradualness that took some of the weight off their shoulders. Young minds which were at once resolute and blithe; Chris, a man who for his years had experienced a wonderful life, who had traveled the world for four summers, and had tried many interesting facets of life, never knew a happier time. Now, his love was told, and it grew by the minute. Though he came here to fish, Annie held him more than the rivers could. They walked hand in hand; their fingers intertwined tightly, along the River Road and hiked some of the paths frequented by Arno and Ennis, and passed some of the sports as they made their way to the best pools. They no longer hid their affection. They liked to walk the pine-needled paths and kick the odd pinecones into the woods. Once, they walked without any fishing tackle along the sunlit banks of Lewis Brook to The Pool, where they rested and kissed for a half hour. Their affection seemed boundless, but there was no sex, and although they had come close at The Pool, there was no mention of it either.

Sometimes on their walks, they talked about the life cycles of the important insects, like the mayflies or the caddises, the stoneflies and the grasshoppers, the spiders and beetles. Chris kept watching for signs that she may be getting overwhelmed by all the entomology, but she showed none. Sometimes they talked about the future. And so, holding hands, they drifted along between shadowy cedars and the old, sunny, open meadows above the town of Roslyn, walking in a waking dream of happiness.

Ben had seen the two lovers on their walks twice, as it happened, once from a distance and another time when the three almost bumped into one another on one of the trails to the West Branch. It was slightly awkward, but only for Ben. As he limped by the couple with a wave of his hand, Annie reached out and hugged Ben and surprised him. Chris stood for a moment, smiling. For him, all was right with the world.

"Benny! Say hello to Chris," she said. She clearly wanted the three to be close, as close friends as she and Ben had become during the summer. Ben was instantly thrown into a quandary – for him all the world wasn't right. It never had been. And although he had gotten the most out of life for having asked less of it, he was now in a place in that old familiar path in the wood where he must make pleasant conversation with the absolute love of his life, and her lover. It wasn't that he didn't like Chris.

"So sorry...I just didn't want to interrupt you folks on your walk," he said.

"Don't be silly!" cried Annie. "We always want to speak with you, Benny." And she gave him another hug. Ben had long ago come to terms with his lot in life. He knew his place in the community and in Annie's world, but it never eliminated the torment of his untold love.

"Do you think you could prepare one of your gourmet meals for Chris some time?" asked Annie. Ben's embarrassed eyes raised up but before he could respond, Chris, who sensed his discomfort, said, "I'm amazed at your *town cabin*, Ben. It's coming along great. All I can figure is you must love building log homes, since you already have a beautiful place up on the river."

"Well, yes...I enjoy it."

"You must...I don't mean to go on about it, but it's so cool, and tasteful. It's so...Roslyn."

"You're too kind," said Ben. "The roof is finished in time for winter only because I had some good help from Annie this summer."

"Did you now!?" Chris draped his arm around Annie's shoulders.

"I didn't do much," she said. "But it was fun learning how a cabin goes together. I helped with some of the purlins." Annie started going on and on about the construction details she learned; how Ben would scribe the notches at the corners of each wall as they went up, one by one; how he used an old pair of calipers he had found in an antique store, and marked the pretty, golden spruce logs with a pencil, and then cut the kerfs with a handsaw about a half-inch apart. He would then knock out the kerfs with the butt of an axe before carefully shaping out the notch with a big gouge.

"When both ends of the log were notched, we would roll the big log over on top of the one below it and, KER-PLUNK!" She was excited even now. "It would fit perfectly, every time!"

Chris was amazed and glanced at Ben, who made his first eye contact back at him, but with a smiling shake of his head, as if to say, "not really."

Chris had long wanted to build his own cabin, and was completely enthralled. Ben was only more embarrassed, although he did love to listen to Annie talk.

"Then Benny would make sure the wall was perfectly plum, and hold the top log in place with these things called 'dogs,' and we'd drill three-quarter inch holes about two inches deep and then spike the logs together with these huge, long spikes – each one a little off-center so the spike wouldn't hit the one below it. Do you know why he would countersink the spikes two inches deep, Chris?" Chris shook his head. "So if the logs shrink over the decades, the spike won't push up into the logs above and make the corner unstable."

"Clever!" said Chris.

"Well, you were sure paying attention," said Ben.

"Are you kidding?" she said. "I *loved* it!"

Ben, perhaps experiencing a weak moment, offered something other than a simple reply to the conversation. "Annie wrote a line from a poem on one of the carrying beams in the rafters," he said. "If you'd like to, you can stop by anytime and write or carve something yourself."

"What?" asked Chris. "Like something out of sight, for posterity?"

"It should be seen, I think, but whatever you want is fine. To me a well-constructed, water-tight building is a house, but the humanism – the *character* is what makes it a home. I don't lock it. Go carve some character into the cabin," he said with a half-smile. "I've got to be going."

"Don't forget a dinner date!" called Annie as Ben limped off. He turned and smiled again and waved.

"Man," said Chris, "is there anything he can't do?"

"Find a wife," said Annie sadly as they started walking.

Their walk took them past the town cabin and they stopped and looked at it from the sidewalk for a while before Chris took Annie's hand and asked her if she minded waiting there for him. Then he walked across the street, went through the cabin door, and looked around the room. He found a step ladder in a corner and added something of himself to a beam. He didn't see Annie's inscription anywhere. Before he left, he admired the fieldstone fireplace, the nice maple floor with tarps and cardboard strewn about protecting the wood, and the wooden pegs holding the timber frame rafters together. When he walked back to the sidewalk, Annie was sitting on the curb. "That took a while," she said wearily, "What did you write?"

"The only thing that came to mind," he said, and they walked back to the farm in the early twilight.

All the next day the rain fell down in sheets, and didn't start to subside until the afternoon. In September the rain in northern Maine can be cold or warm, soft or hard, drizzling straight down or driving sideways. This day it was cold, and it washed away the last few mosquitoes of the season, and made the air smell sweet and fresh. Chris spent most of the day sitting in the living room, reading in one of the overstuffed chairs (he was careful not to sit in Mr. Nielson's favorite chair) and talking with Annie. When in the afternoon her father came in to read the paper, Annie excused herself to start supper.

John started the conversation, "Are you catchin' many fish this trip?"

"Oh, we've caught a few...I'm sure you know the fishing's a bit different in the fall," Chris replied.

"Ayuh," John confirmed. He lit his pipe and thought for a moment, staring at the empty fireplace. "You know, I think it's cold enough for a little fire tonight. What do you think?"

"Absolutely, I'd like to do some more reading tonight, and a nice fire would be great."

John Nielson hoisted himself from his favorite chair, locked his pipe in his mouth with a good bite and strode off to the ell between the kitchen and the barn and came back with a canvas bag filled with four large sticks of firewood and a handful of kindling. He arranged the logs in the hearth with the biggest placed on top of the kindling. He then lit the kerosene-soaked stone from the Cape Cod lighter and shoved it underneath the cedar kindling. Within two minutes the fire was crackling, popping and warm. It lit up half the room and gave a nice, golden glow. It was wonderful.

John had settled back down into his chair when Chris finally spoke.

"I'd been hoping for a chance to speak with you, sir." Annie's father was caught off guard for a moment, and said nothing. He wanted to choose his words carefully. If it was about what he thought, this boy might be around him for a long time; maybe for years, maybe from here on out. And before he could ask him what it was he wanted to say, Chris fired away.

"You know, Mr. Nielson, *sir*, (ahem) Annie and I have been spending some time together. (John knew that.) And we've grown quite fond of each other." Chris hoped John would show some sort of emotion, perhaps say something—show concern, happiness, acceptance, show *something*. But the old farmer just sat there, stunned by the analysis of the moment. He knew that as of that moment, sitting in his comfortable chair by the warm, sweet fire that everything would change. Everything would be different. Yes, he might possibly be alone; he might have to try to run the farm by himself. He might become very, very lonely. He thought of these things not because he was overly concerned with his own state of affairs, but because he had been preparing for this for years. Annie's remarkable beauty was not lost on him. Here was the first time a young man was speaking to him about "the subject." The bottom line was as it is for all fathers; Annie was his little girl and his only real concern was for her happiness.

But still, he said nothing. He put the ball squarely in Chris's hands. Seemingly always comfortable in every situation, Chris was now starting to feel the weight of the conversation. He wasn't sweating, but he understood how important his profession of commitment would be to both Annie and to her father. Chris either had to speak, or sit in an increasingly uncomfortable silence.

"Well, sir, I just wanted you to know that I...well, I suppose I wanted you to know how I feel about Annie, and this sounds a little old-fashioned, but my intentions are honorable. I'm not planning on proposing to Annie tomorrow, but I do love her and I wanted you to know I respect her, and you."

Annie's dad looked long and hard at Chris, sat back in his chair a little farther, took his pipe out of his mouth and with a sure look of resignation said, "I suppose you should call me John."

The two talked for quite a while about Chris's graduate school, some of the places he had traveled to, and a lot about Annie, and Annie pretended not to listen from the kitchen. As if both men realized they had covered enough for the time being, they simply stopped talking and stared at the fire. Chris felt strangely at home. He felt at home, he felt comfortable, he felt in love, and he was happy.

Annie and Chris knew they were together now.

That evening, long after John had gone to bed, the living room and the crackling fire would be theirs alone. They would sit together in the same overstuffed chair he sat in earlier when he spoke to her father. Chris drew her down so that she sat in his lap and within his arms. Then it was lips upon lips till he lifted his head at last and said, "I suppose every young man and his brother in Roslyn is in love with you?"

She didn't answer no, but rather, "I don't want any of them. I'm very happy with you, here, like this...by the fire."

He looked at her lovingly and started stroking the full column of her neck. "You are the loveliest person I've ever seen." He passed his hand all around her face, her neck, around beneath her chin and down to the soft hollow above her breastbone.

She closed her eyes as his caressing hand sought other parts of her, but she gently held his hand and stopped him. She wanted him, more than anything, but as if apologizing for the rejection she spoke with her heart: "Not here."

"Honey, if you...at some point ...well, I'm ready if you are."

She was silent for a moment. While she did not say yes, she did not say no. She was smiling to herself, defeated by her own desires.

Ever the gentleman, he spoke again. "If you're not ready, that's perfectly all right." She was overcome with emotion and said, "I love you so much."

He paused for a moment and then asked in a hushed voice, "Tonight?"

"Are you sure of what you want?"

Chris looked at her lovingly. "I only want you. All of you, in every way."

In their beds they both lay awake. Annie stared at the ceiling driven awake with anticipation, anxiety, desire – all of this wrapped in a tense ball that was blanketed by a happiness she hadn't felt before. Chris tossed and turned and tried everything to direct his mind. He thought about fishing, hoping to fall asleep, and ended up thinking about fishing for salmon with Annie. He tried remembrances of travels past, and only imagined sharing the same experiences with his new love. Nothing worked.

The house was quiet. Annie thought she heard a step in the hall. Her breathing deepened.

"Are you awake, Annie?" There was a yes that was hardly audible, and she received him with open arms. She felt his athletic body next to her and she breathed in his smell, a wonderful smell she hadn't fully noticed before. Her heart raced in the darkness. Lying at her side he smoothed back the beautiful blonde hair from her brow so he could kiss her brow, and cheek, and lips. He gently kissed the whole length of her arm, the elbow, her shoulder and found her breasts. "Annie, I've wondered at times, am I the first to be with you?"

She was a bit embarrassed by her inexperience, but with heavy breath said, "Yes."

"Do you want to now?" he asked.

"Whatever you want."

"I just...I don't want to hurt you, honey."

She did not answer but only drew him closer and waited, her chest heaving. There was some pain, and she gasped. He tried to stay very still and stroked her soft hair to comfort her. Slowly he produced for her the mounting ecstasy she had never known. "Oh, Chris, I do love you!" At once he gasped, "Annie, I love *you!*"

They lay there together hot, breathless, and quiet in the dark. And in the darkness, Chris could not see the tear roll down her cheek, but he could taste it when he kissed her face and felt alarm. "Honey...are you all right?" She just nodded her head yes and then sniffed once while another tear rolled down her cheek, and she simply whispered, "I'm happy."

An hour later he left her bed. He said in a half-whisper, "Annie, do you want me to come back here again tomorrow?"

"Of course." The pleasure, the ecstasy was too much for her to refuse him. After all, she had dreamt of this for years. He kissed her and left her lying alone, happy, pensive.

What price had she paid for this love? She knew of girls in town who had had sex with their boyfriends only to be "ditched," after so many promises. She prepared herself for Chris to be the same, although she couldn't imagine it. Or was the love and commitment there all along, and this night was the natural progression of things? Annie came to tears a couple of times during the night, lying alone on her bed in the dark.

In the morning they were back in the daylight and the world of Roslyn was as if nothing important had happened. Annie was doing her customary household chores; John Nielson was harvesting winter squash and ornamental gourds in the front field, cursing the deer again that had nibbled ruinous grooves out of the pumpkins in the adjacent field. Ennis Gray and Doc Warren strolled down the road on their way to the trail head that leads up to the top of Thornton Hill. Doc was rambling on about stoneflies as Ennis waved a friendly wave at John, who stopped cursing only enough to smile and wave back.

But Chris was different. The early morning sequence over the last few weeks for him included the realization that he was more in love with Annie than the day before, and that he was doing the right thing, and however life turned out for him professionally the two would find a way to be together, as husband and wife. But today, *this* morning it was different. He knew he had to find "the way" to make everything work for them, and for John. There was no turning back now, and he loved how he felt. He embraced the commitment, and he felt perfect inside. Since he was a boy, if he felt badly, or excited, or happy or sad, he would often find solace in the current of a stream or a river, and would often find peace or encouragement in the life that the river gives. This morning, he left early for the West Branch. He wanted to stand in the flow of the water. He wanted to watch the insects emerge, and the muskrat scurry along the shoreline, and the fish rising, and to scream to the river world what a lucky man he was indeed.

Annie would never be the same. Her range of emotions after he left her bed that night went in every direction of the compass. She always felt she had "kept it all together" more than most girls her own age, and had, for someone not traveled, embodied a worldly-wise sensibility regarding everyday issues. She kept trying to tell herself that her emotional rollercoaster ride was probably normal. Keep it together, she thought, before Dad comes in for breakfast.

She did conceal her new life from all who might see, but she walked with a different bearing. It was as if in an instant she possessed a weightier perception of life's considerations, a subtle maturity different from the mature demeanor the girl from yesterday had always had.

When her father did finally come into the kitchen and washed some of the front field off his hands and face, she said, "I'll have some eggs ready for you in just a minute."

She knew her father, and she knew he suspected nothing. Yes, she had overheard some of Chris's conversation with him the day before, but it was relatively non-committal.

He turned around from the sink and leaned against the counter, looked at her lovingly, wiping his hands dry.

"No," he said softly, "I'll make my own breakfast. It's time I started doing for myself, anyways." He had a slight smile in one corner of his lips, and his eyes had a soft, strained look like those times when he was overtired.

The mature, worldly-wise, smart and tough young woman threw down her washcloth and said, "Oh, Daddy!" She wrapped her arms around his neck and cried a happy, sad and scared cry. John Nielson tried to fake a laugh but his throat was suddenly sore and it sounded more like a suppressed cough, as he gently patted her back and said, "Everything's going to be just fine, Annie Girl. It'll be just fine."

THIRTEEN

Chris made his way along the river bank, jumping from boulder to boulder in his waders with his fly rod held out behind him in case he stumbled. If he did lose his footing, the rod tip wouldn't jab into the ground or stab a tree and snap off. So giddy from the turn his life had taken, he felt as though he was walking on air.

He worked his way down to the same bend pool Tom had fished last spring. Chris sat on the same boulder where he had watched his friend land his salmon and where he had thought so long and hard about Annie. He marveled at how only a few months ago he was almost annoyed at how that beautiful girl had completely unsettled him and now, he was determined to make her his wife.

He knew the water level would be much lower than when they were there last spring, making the bend pool fish differently. The Class IV rapids below the pool were now Class III. There were a few ledges he could work his way onto and cast which were under water until a month ago. He had fished from those spots before late in the season and had done well. Two years ago, he caught his best salmon, just over five pounds on one of Ennis's Nine-Three streamers. On most days, Chris would rather fish dry flies. If the fish weren't looking up he would usually turn to nymphs. Occasionally, he would try streamers if the water looked promising for holding particularly *big* fish. As he told Annie, bigger fish often require more sustenance than do little fish, so they are more likely to eat bait fish to augment their diet of bugs.

He sat for a long time on the tall boulder. His mind, normally sharp, was now filled with connected but random thoughts. He thought about when he first met Annie; then he watched the river for signs of rising fish. He thought about how his friends and family would take to his marrying a girl from a farm in northern Maine who hadn't even been to college. They would love her the moment they met her and they would instantly see how capable she was. Then he noticed a large zebra caddis flutter by. *A size twelve, maybe,* he thought. He remembered the first time he fished with Annie on Lewis Brook, and how quickly she learned to cast—twice as fast as anyone else he'd taught. Then he focused back on the river in front of him, and he remembered how nervous he was last spring, watching Tom fish the bend pool when the water was higher – the big, dangerous current so close to where he had stood. In an instant, his mind went to Doc Warren. He wondered what he would think of his marrying Annie. Doc was one of the people who helped John raise her after her mother died. Adelis Nielson—he wondered what she was like. Adelis, he thought...where'd that name come from? He had met a few girls in Germany named Adelaide, and there is a city in Australia with the same spelling. Maybe Adelis is a variation from that name. Then he watched the pool again, looking for any rises.

Man! he thought to himself. *So this is what ADHD is like. Or what love is like.*

Chris stepped out onto the very same ledge Tom had fished from. With the water level down so much, the ledge now tapered out into the river about fifteen feet farther than last April. Half way out he stopped to try the deep, dark eddy below the ledge, where the foam on the surface told the tale of the backward current, where nymphs and terrestrial insects would be floating by. He tied on a large golden stonefly nymph and fastened a brightly-colored foam indicator to the line at the butt end of the leader, near to where it attaches to the fly line. It's legal at the West Branch to use two flies, which most anglers do, but Chris preferred to fish one fly at a time. He never said why, except that he once told Tom he could "work the fly better." He payed out about thirty feet of line, letting the fly drift downstream into the eddy while he surveyed the water one more time. The main current was farther out off the point of the ledge, about thirty feet from where he stood, coming hard from his left. He took a few more steps, being careful not to step too close to the right where the rock ledge dropped off into the deep eddy. He inched his way out to the point of the ledge, leaving his fly line in the water downstream. Here he had only eighteen inches of rock to perch on, but there were two good depressions in the ledge to put his feet into, his left foot in front of his right, so his stance looked like he was in mid-stride. From there he could cast out into the fast-moving main current.

Fish lived in that spot. He knew because he had caught some nice salmon from there more than a few times over the years. He knew also it would be a difficult cast. Quartering upstream against the constant, stiff wind, it would require an upstream, left-hand reach cast (*against* the breeze). As soon as the fly touched the water's surface, he would need to mend the line upstream at least twice for any chance of a decent drift. He checked his footing twice on the narrow rock and then made a couple of false casts. Haul the line, pick it up, forward cast and then bring it back too soon to keep the fly airborne, the line cutting through the air like the branch of a weeping willow caught in a gale. He glanced again at his feet while he false cast the fly and his stance seemed okay.

The fourth false cast he let fly. He reached to the left and the line was deposited upstream a little from the leader. He quickly made two upstream mends and before he could start to fish the fly line was sweeping downstream in a wide arc, pulling the leader and the fly with it much too fast. Even a suicidal salmon wouldn't have eaten the nymph with that drift. Chris pulled in the line and pinched onto the leader some split shot about two feet above the fly to try and get the nymph down a little deeper but it would only make the cast harder. Trying to cast a wide loop to prevent the fly, split shot, and indicator from getting tangled or, more likely, a wind knot in the leader, Chris tried the same spot along the seam of the main current. On the second cast he watched the indicator intently as it bobbed and tumbled through the waves and floated swiftly downriver. It wasn't perfect, but was a better drift and he was surprised when the indicator shot upstream against the current. He raised the rod tip quickly but gently and felt the weight of the salmon in the cork in his hand. There were two quick pulses in the length of the rod and then— slack! The fish was gone. Chris wasn't disappointed; it was just part of the game. He had hooked and lost more fish than he could count, and would probably lose that many more. He simply hauled in the line, lifted the rod tip again and made two more of the same cast, but with no luck. That was enough.

He turned his attention to below the rock ledge where the eddy curls back around and rejoins the main current of the river. The foamy seam where the two waters join becomes a feeding lane for salmon which wait in the slack water, feeding when they feel like it. Chris shifted his feet around on the narrow ledge and faced straight down the river, right in line with the feeding lane. He made certain of his balance on the rock. He couldn't help but notice how pretty Mount Katahdin looked, looming over the river valley, not twenty miles away. He flipped the rod tip and executed a sweet little roll cast only a short distance in front of him, landing perfectly into the seam of water. As the indicator floated away Chris simply payed out line, slowly enough to keep a reasonable "tightness" in the line so he could set the hook if he needed to, but fast enough so that he didn't alter the natural drift of the fly underwater. Nothing. He tried it again a bit farther out into the main current. The fly didn't even have time to sink when the indicator quickly darted across the current towards the main part of the river. "Oh!" he said aloud, and quickly set the hook in spite of not being ready. At the same time the hook bit into the fish's mouth, the salmon shot from the water and his whole body was in midair for a split second. Not a monster, but a nice fish. He was into the main current now, and Chris knew his only chance of landing him was to get him on the reel as fast as possible. He held the rod tip up (but not too high) so the strain was squarely on the butt section, the part of the rod built for fighting fish.

Holding the line with his right index finger, he grabbed the slack line which was dangling in the water at his feet and looped it around his right pinky finger. This created a little tension to reel against, which made the line fill the reel more evenly, preventing a tangle on the spool. Studying the fish,

Chris reeled the line in through his pinky as fast as possible. Twice, he had to stop reeling to give the salmon some line. Once he got him on the reel he checked the drag and then let the line go. Nothing happened at first, but when Chris pulled the rod upstream with authority, the reel screamed for a few seconds as the fish bolted and took line with it. The salmon, which seemed larger now, tried hard to work his way farther into the heavy current and into deeper water. But Chris worked him hard; he kept applying pressure on the fish, first this way, and then another. Once more, he jumped from the water and the experienced angler got a better look at him; he was happy to see the silver landlocked shining in the September sun.

Chris tried to bring the fish in quickly now that he had tired some. He didn't want to play the fish so hard and so long that he would have a hard time recovering. The young man horsed him a little at the end of the fight. Once he got him into the big eddy, Chris pulled the landing net from the magnet on the back of his fly vest and bent down, carefully, guiding the fish into it. Most salmon are beautiful, but this fish was exceptionally fine. He was fat and strong and had a healthy look to him. Chris noticed a long, curved scar on the fish's back, just behind the dorsal fin; it looked to be from a kingfisher, or possibly an osprey. This fish had fought for its life successfully when he was younger. He had fought hard again today. Chris tried to keep him in the water as he removed the barbless nymph from the middle of his upper lip. He snapped a quick photo of him with his waterproof camera, but he knew he would remember this fish. It wasn't huge, and it wasn't a unique contest, but this triumph occurred on a special day for Chris. He let the net dangle from its lanyard, and gently released the salmon back into the eddy. The pretty fish slowly swam away, none worse for the wear. At least Chris hoped so.

Chris stood for a moment, happy to be doing what he felt he was born to do, looking up at the mountain and the thousands of sparkling silver waves as the river scurried down the valley. His thoughts once again turned to Annie. *I wish she was here,* he thought. He paused for a moment more. Having made his decision, he started wondering how he would propose to her. *It should be on the river somewhere, but not here...Lewis Brook! At The Pool! That would be perfect. But it has to be a perfect day. And it has to be before I head back home.* A big caddis fly fluttered by his face, and he tried to catch it in his baseball hat, but missed. He felt so small and alone there, standing on a little ledge in the middle of a big river, like he was in a calendar photo, but from the inside looking out, watching a month's worth of the world going by. It was days like this, alone on a moving body of water with only nature to hold him, that were his days of worship. He was in his church. He didn't know it, but it was the same church Ben attended.

Below the ledge and the big eddy was the steep downhill grade where the big water picked up speed and turbulent power. He knew he could reach a nice run about 100 yards downstream where usually some bigger salmon would be holding, especially in the fall. He worked his way along the ledge towards shore. He stepped confidently along the wet ledge. Half way across he was still thirty feet from shore. He kept his balance but when he took a step with his left foot, he felt the rubber-soled wading boot slip quickly down the drop-off of the downstream side of the ledge and into the water. His leg disappeared into the eddy well past his knee and it violently threw him off balance, and he was tossed forward by the momentum of the fall. His fly rod flew from his hand and landed into the water on the opposite side of the rock. He tried to catch himself by throwing his right foot forward onto a section of the ledge that was just underwater. That boot also found no purchase and his whole body was thrown into the big eddy, awkwardly for such an athletic man. He landed with a big splash, and was instantly underwater. He spun himself around, trying to grab hold of the ledge. He touched the rock with his fingertips, but found no hand-hold. Both his hands were reaching, grasping, clutching for anything to hold, but the weight of his wet fly vest and clothes made him feel like a three hundred pound man. *Oh, God...this is bad!* raced through his mind. He realized his waders were filled up with water and he paddled hard for the surface. He paddled, flailed, reached and fought and stared to the sky and saw nothing but bubbles and sheets of light. Losing his breath, he still could think clearly and he knew his grasping hands were four feet below the surface, and that the filled-up waders were pulling him under even more. The eddy was deep enough that he found no solid footing. Chris was wheezing and coughing, and he was losing his breath. In the slow motion, rumbling explosion of liquid darkness, he quickly became exhausted. By the time the force of the water in the eddy had pushed him into the main current, he had stopped thinking of the water, or of his waders, or of the bubbles.

His mind turned inexplicably to other thoughts. He was struggling less now, just his arms and feet moving gently about in the water – not moved by the current – but still under his own power, as if he were still fighting for his life but barely moving, as though he was weightless. Visions of Annie flashed in front of him, and he worried what would happen to her now. He felt her anguish inside him and it made him vomit. Then he saw his parents, then his friends. Calmness came over him, and he suddenly felt unafraid. He could see without vision, and there was no sound. He had full knowledge that death was upon him, and that any further physical effort was useless. He became resigned to his fate. The most loving and caring memories flooded his mind. Everything he saw was bathed in a bright, bluish light. It was as if he could feel the light. In sharp details he had a more vivid view of the water, the rocks, of the river, of *himself*. He was struck by the peace and comfort of it. He became more aware, or perhaps, conscious. It was as though he was a new...self. He was a bundle of experiences now that was his former self.

He could see Earth, bathed in the same bluish light and all of his considerations in life; pain, loss, happiness, wishes were being sloughed away. He no longer owned any desires. His time with Annie was a part of this bundle. He was led by a light to an illuminated room without walls, where he knew upon entering he would understand his personal history, his existence, and his reason for living. He somehow knew he would be with all the people who had been an important part of his reality of earth. It was beautiful.

Chris's fear for Annie was comforted by the newfound knowledge that no matter what anguish she might experience in her life, and no matter the trials, she would ultimately feel the same tranquil love and happiness and painlessness. That was enough for him, and he surrendered.

FOURTEEN

John Nielson was sitting in his Adirondack chair on the porch that evening, just smoking his pipe and thinking how happy he was that almost everything for the season was harvested, and wondered if Ben's idea of focusing on garlic was as smart as it seemed. He had never planted anything in the late fall before, but maybe it would be just the ticket to keep the farm going. There would be the revenue from the fishing guests in spring and fall, *but if Annie moves away, I certainly won't keep guests.*

John thought he heard a car door out on the main road, and a moment later Doc Warren walked up the driveway with two other men whom he didn't recognize. Annie also heard the car, and looked out the kitchen window in time to see the three men approach the porch. As they did, she saw her father stand up to greet them. It looked to her like Arno introduced the two other men to her dad and he shook their hands. They looked official...*I wonder who they are?* Maybe they're from the Farm Service Administration—they had helped with the farm some years ago, she thought, and her father had a good relationship with the agent. But she had never seen these men before.

Annie watched through the window as she kept washing dishes. As soon as Arno started to speak, she saw her father clumsily reach out to his left and grab hold of the white timber pillar that held up the porch roof. His shoulders slumped and his head fell forward for a moment. Then he turned his head around and with a pained, pitiful face and looked directly towards the kitchen window.

She hadn't seen her father look like that since her Mom passed years before. *What's going on?! Someone's hurt! Was it Benny? Or maybe Ennis God forbid...or...was it Chris? Or has Dad gotten into some kind of trouble with the farm and has kept it from me? But if that's the case, why is Arno here?* Thoughts started to race through her head. Her father turned back to the men and said something. The two strangers walked off and Doc and John spoke for another few seconds before starting for the door. Annie braced herself for any sort of news, took off her apron and sat at the kitchen table. Her father opened the door and let Doc in first. Arno's lips were pursed, and he tried hard to smile, but couldn't. He sat down next to Annie and her father slumped into the chair opposite her.

"I have something to tell you, Annie, darlin'." He paused for what seemed like a long time. "It's not good." They looked at each other squarely in the eyes. Hers started to tear up. He reached across the table and held her hand, gently with his bent, gnarled fingers. She took a deep breath. She knew now that it was very bad. She could see that her father's kind face, ruddy and stained by the sun, was now soft, and sad, and scared. His eyes didn't leave hers. After her deep breath, her father winced a little and nodded once slowly. Arno slid his chair a few inches closer to hers and folded his hands on the table in front of him.

"There's been an accident," he said. "It's Chris." Annie felt a shudder rake her body, and she sucked in air and gasped. She saw the tears well up in her father's eyes for the first time in her life. John grew up in a generation in which men didn't cry. When her mother passed away, her father cried in private but she could always read his eyes and tell when he had been. And she could read them now. A tear rolled down his leathery cheek. Her free hand clasped her mouth. Doc put his arm around her trembling shoulders.

"One of Ennis's guides found him below the Big Eddy. He must have slipped on the rocks somewhere above the rapids." She was sobbing now, but still waiting, attentive. "He's gone, honey."

"No!! No!" She cried loud enough to be heard from a very long way. She wailed and dropped her head, crying inconsolably. "No, God! Not Chris!" She rained tears now. John stood up and hugged her from across the table while Arno held her and rubbed her back gently. She cried and cried till she almost lost her breath. She wailed for more than ten minutes before she started to breathe more regularly and the two men never moved. Even Doc Warren, the worldly physician who had seen it all in his thirty years of practice, wept.

"I...I need to lie down," she sobbed. Doc and her father helped her up and walked her to the parlor and laid her down on the small sofa next to the overstuffed chairs.

John knelt by the couch and lovingly stroked her hand while repeatedly shaking his head. As her breathing returned to near normal in between the sobs of agony, he finally spoke. "It's a cruel turn for you, honey. He was a good boy. (More louder sobs of agony.) It won't seem like it now, my sweet girl, but everything gets better with time."

"Daddy," she said in between sobs, "I can't feel anything. It's like a blackness."

"I know, honey, I know," he said. "You'll need to rest now. But I'll stay with you." He squeezed her hand tightly and she lifted her eyes to his. "You need to understand this," he said, "Annie...can you hear what I'm saying?" She looked up at him through the tears and nodded. "You are *never* alone."

Doc left a while later after promising to come by in the morning. Annie stayed on the couch with her hand over her eyes, crying, for three hours until exhausted, she finally fell asleep, and John sat in the chair near her head and watched over her.

Annie slept on that couch for the entire night and her father never left her side. She emerged from that deep sleep into a silence of days. Rather than talk about Chris, she threw herself into her work, helping with the farm chores, cleaning, putting up firewood, whatever she could find. John tried to get her to discuss it, and so did Doc, but she wasn't ready.

Almost a week had passed before Arno and Ennis came to the farm to tell John and Annie that Chris's body would be returned to Roslyn in two days and interned at the little cemetery in town. Doc told them that the angler's parents called him that day at his office. Doc said they knew very well their son's love for the town and for its people, and they were sure he would prefer to be buried here.

Annie and John held hands again and she held herself together, for the moment.

"There's more," said Doc. "His father told me Chris had told them all about you Annie. They didn't have a phone number or an address for you. They believe he wanted to...well...they hope to meet you when they come for the service." Annie wiped the tears from her cheeks and nodded approvingly. As they got up to leave, Ennis spoke for the first time.

"We all love you, Annie."

Doc added as they reached the door, "You should go to Ben; he's quite worried about you. Might be good for you to talk to someone your own age. Anyway, that boy's a better healer than I am. I'm sure it'd be good for you."

******

Autumn was in full swing when Chris's service took place. They buried him near the back of the cemetery under a small maple tree, only a few hundred yards from where the West Branch flows slowly through town, resting before it makes its final run to the sea. Just behind the headstone, the back border of the cemetery falls down a bank where little Southwest Brook trickles by on its way to the river. It's small, but even in summer you can hear it babbling from the maple tree. His father thought Chris would like that.

Annie hadn't had a chance to meet his parents yet, and they waited for her out by the road at the end of the service. Everyone there either went home, or to the Riverdriver. Annie was left alone at the grave. She was amazed at how she felt...she was sad, but...okay. She was happy to have him here, in Roslyn. The stone was simple. It read;

Christopher Jayne Phelps
Died 1997   Aged 26 years
-Ah, but a man's reach should exceed his grasp,
Or what's a Heaven for?

Annie walked up to the stately couple waiting for her. Chris's father was taller than his son and just as handsome. His mother was elegant and seemed to be much more relaxed than Annie imagined. She felt badly that she didn't own a black dress for the service, but no one seemed to mind. They met with hugs, sad smiles, and cordiality and Mr. Phelps introduced himself and his wife as Richard and Sandy, and all three sat on one of the wooden benches next to the gate that led out onto the sidewalk.

Chris's mom spoke first, and the most. "My God, child…Chris said you were beautiful, but I had no idea." Annie shook her head very slightly, as if to disagree.

"We want to thank you for loving him." Annie started to weep. Sandy Phelps held one of Annie's hands and gently stroked her hair. "Listen to me, dear; a month ago Chris told us that you'd given him the happiest days of his life. I want you…*we* want you to remember that forever. And dear, he told us so much about you – whatever happens; I know you will have a great life." Mrs. Phelps paused and looked at their hands clasped together. "I want you to remember this also: if we can do anything for you…*anything*, God, please let us do it. We feel you are a part of us, Annie."

The stoic resignation the two grieving parents had was an inspiration to Annie. All three walked the long walk to the farm where the Phelpses were introduced to John Nielson and shown the farm. Along the way, they talked and reminisced and Richard even told a few of his favorite things Chris had done as a youngster. At the farm they shared coffee, and Richard seemed genuinely interested about the workings of the farm. He was fascinated by the tentative plans to experiment with garlic production. After coffee, he and John walked the top field and tried to talk farming, but ended up weeping together. They shared contact information, and there was a tearful parting.

The service, the fact that Chris would be resting nearby, the visit with the Phelpses and the time spent together were wonderfully healing for Annie. She started to mend.

She still did not sing while doing chores as she had always done, but now, as time went by, she did start to hum a little. John took it as a good sign. Father and daughter were closer than ever, and as the days turned into weeks, Annie's heart began to mend.

As autumn surrendered to winter's winds, the heart-sick girl decided to take the walk up Lewis Brook before the ice started to form. It was a lonely walk. As she got to The Pool, her heart sank more than usual as the flood of memories came rushing back. She sat on the rock where Chris had helped her catch her first brook trout. She remembered it like it was yesterday, yet it *seemed* like years ago. At first, she thought it might have been a mistake to come back to that spot, but she remembered what Ben had said to her the last time they had a chance to speak. It was a brief conversation only a short time after Chris had died, but in farming, timing is everything, and Benny had arrived on October fifteenth with a truckload of seed garlic for John to plant. He wouldn't let Annie's dad pay for it. While Annie separated and graded the cloves, Ben approached her and asked if she was all right. She nodded a sad "yes", and said she was having a hard time forgetting. She didn't mean forgetting Chris, of course, she meant not dwelling on how very close she was to such a perfect life. Ben was short with her for the first and only time.

"You mustn't forget...any of it," he said. "All those moments you had with him are experiences you need to hold onto. Those things, along with everything else in your life, make you...*you*. Instead of dwelling on the loss, you've got to eventually take everything positive from your time together, and thank God that you knew and loved him." Annie told him then that his words sounded like something Chris would have said, and it had made her feel a tiny bit better.

He was right, she thought, and now, there on the rock at The Pool, she began for the first time to think of a future without her love. But before she left, she lay down on the rock and looked up through the branches at the cold October sky, and while the brook babbled and chortled at her feet, she asked of Chris, "Do you feel me, wherever you are? Do you feel the love I still have for you?"

She felt a strange warmth come over her on that cold rock, under the dark cedar branches. She inexplicably felt an appreciation for living in such a wonderful town, with such beautiful people. She was thankful for the support her father had given her and the same for Arno and Ennis. She felt especially thankful for her friendship with Ben, whom she knew she could call on whenever she needed.

The next morning, she had an overwhelming desire to talk to somebody other than her father. She walked down the river road and into town to see if Ben would be working on the "town cabin," as she called it. Every time she went there, she still was struck with wonder as to why Ben wanted to build it. Sure, he enjoyed the work, but his cabin on the river was so inviting and quaint. It was obviously an investment for Ben. Annie was sure he would sell it to some sports to use for the summer. She supposed he would use the money to travel. She envied him, now that she knew him well.

She saw his old International in the dooryard and called in the open front door. The new cabin was nearly finished now, and still smelled wonderfully of newly worked wood and oakum. The roof and floor were done, and there were canvas tarps laid around to protect the floor's finish. The cabin was one capacious room with cathedral ceilings. In the very back, there were two small enclosed rooms; one, a small bathroom, and in the opposite corner was an empty room with the door propped open. Perfectly placed between the little rooms along the back wall was a crescent-shaped bar – or what looked like a bar.

"Annie!" Ben emerged from the room that wasn't a bathroom.

"Ben! This place looks great! You've done a lot lately."

"Yes...well, it'll snow soon." Ben glanced up at the finished roof. There were no chairs, so Ben motioned for her to lean against one of the saw horses. He sat next to her but as his butt hit the board he sprang back up. "Oh! There's something I wanted you to see," he said. He led her by the hand a bit farther into the great room and turned her around facing the front door and motioned for her to look up. Along one of the purlins was Chris's inscription, all in upper case letters;

"LIKE ONE GONE MAD I HUGGED THE GROUND,
 I RAISED MY QUIVERING ARMS ON HIGH,
 I LAUGHED AND LAUGHED INTO THE SKY."

She put her hand over her mouth and read it silently, and shed yet another tear. Her other hand reached out for Ben's. She had forgotten about this. She was wondering what to say about it when Ben, still looking at the quote said, "I think it's cool as hell. He wrote it with one of my carpenter's pencils, and then cut it out with a knife. You can see the outline of the pencil lead. If you like it, I want to polyurethane over it before it fades or gets rubbed off somehow."

"Oh, yes...I love it!" She read it through again. "I feel like I've seen it before..."

"It's Edna St. Vincent Millay ...from Renascence."

Annie sniffed, smiled and glanced from the inscription to around the cabin, and then a quick glance back at the purlin. Then she turned to Ben, whose face was still radiating delight at seeing her. "I came for a reason, Ben," she began.

"I'm just going to say it," she said aloud. "I miss you, and I...I was wondering if I could come see you soon."

His big, handsome brown eyes opened wide with surprise. "Of course." He said it with an inflection that suggested she needn't have asked, and it made her comfortable again. He always made her comfortable.

"Chris cared a lot for you, and I could use someone to talk to...about everything."

"Yes, yes...let's have a long talk. Why don't you come over tomorrow night?" She felt him squeeze her hand playfully as he said with a half-wink, "I'll cook."

"Thank you, Ben," she sighed. She didn't realize they were still holding hands.

******

So the next evening she walked down the little brick path from the driveway, through the perennial garden, put to bed for the winter and towards the sweet little cabin. It was an unseasonably warm autumn evening. She remembered how lovely the impatiens looked in the window boxes last summer, and how the perennials seemed as if they were growing there naturally. The smaller plants were in the front, but it didn't look contrived, and the colors and the foliage seemed to blend so well together. She also remembered last summer, when Ben had told her that the secret to designing a perennial garden was to use the building blocks of atmosphere; light, color, texture, and progression. There was a tiny table and two Adirondack chairs in the garden she had never noticed before.

She reached for the bell (an actual bell, with a string and a clapper) but the door opened before she could ring it. It startled her for a moment.

"Oh! Hi!" she said.

"Come in, Annie." He wanted to call her "dear" or, "darling," as he always had in his thoughts. He had a bright fire in the big fireplace. On the coffee table in front of the fire was an opened wine bottle, two little glasses, a bowl of nuts and some sliced cheese and crackers.

"Benny, you haven't gone to any trouble for me, have you?"

"Cheese, wine and crackers! You think that's going to trouble?" He was smiling at her.

"No, I guess not, actually," she looked back at the table. "But it's lovely."

"Well, if you like that then you're going to *love* the roast duck in a blackberry flambé."

"Benjamin!"

"I just thought you might like a good meal to go with the conversation," he said with a mock defensiveness. He didn't tell her that he had rushed home from the town cabin the day before to thaw out one of the ducklings. He had spent most of the afternoon getting ready for her arrival.

They ate the duck, which was perfect, and the asparagus and the roasted garlic and the saffron almond rice. Annie loved it all. *My God, this guy is an amazing cook!* After supper, they sat together on the couch by the fire and talked. They talked for a long time, and as the evening wore on and it got dark, Ben got up to light some candles in some brass candlesticks on the mantle. As he lit the second one he bumped the stick and it almost upset the candle. He glanced at Annie who was watching him. She was curled up on the couch now, looking perfectly comfortable. "Smooth," she said.

Ben answered as if it always happened the same way, "This one doesn't hold a candle to the other."

"Ha, ha," she mock laughed.

As usual, Annie soon found herself at ease with him. She found it was a relief to describe the feelings and emotions she had experienced over the past weeks.

The conversation became all hers and Ben listened, very quietly. He would nod in agreement, or shake his head. He wanted to know everything. Some of it was intense, and some was difficult to hear, but he loved being with her. Evenings such as this one they had spent together during the summer were the best nights of his life. He missed spending time with her. But this was all about her, and the trauma she was trying to come to terms with. They had entered into a process, one they were trying to work through together.

She told him of how Chris had admired Ben's self-reliance, no, not self-reliance but rather his long lists of accomplishments and expertise. How Chris had marveled at Ben's craftsmanship and, with a sweep of her hand, how he loved the cabin they sat in. How he had hoped someday to build one like it.

She worried about mentioning his afflictions. "I know you're self-conscious about your back, Benny, but Chris admired you for your triumphs."

"Overcoming one's own deformities can have its own reward...or overcoming one's own disasters," he said looking intently at her. "Annie, I think we've been through enough, you and I, so we can talk about anything. That includes my physical problems. You can ask me any questions you want. I'd rather be with you and answer difficult questions than not be with you. So, fire away." He was amazed at his own words and he felt great about opening up.

But she only asked one thing. She cared deeply for him, and she respected him above all else, save her father. She asked him the only thing she cared about. She sat on the couch, her wine glass nearly empty and she looked at him quite lovingly. She could see that he was happy to have her there, but she could not feel the hopeless, unspoken love flowing towards her.

"Are you in pain...Ben?"

He wanted to tell her no, that physically he had no more pain than anybody else and how he only felt the same aches and pains associated with common injuries and strains. It did not occur to him to tell her that he mostly had a somewhat limited range of motion in his back and neck, and that he had a slight leg length discrepancy which altered his gait, even though *that* is what people focused on. But he didn't. He reached somewhere deep in his guts and dredged up the courage to say what he felt about pain.

"Not...when I'm with you. Here, like this." In an instant he knew it was too much, and he had ruined what friendship they had built. He felt sick. But she only smiled, and reached out and touched his knee to reassure him that it was all right.

FIFTEEN

Snow came to the valley just before Christmas, and it came hard. There was a blizzard on the twentieth of December, and Doc Warren said it was the worst one to hit them in twenty years. The sports were home in their city houses, and most of Roslyn hunkered down for the winter. The spruce and the cedar trees looked heartwarming, not cold, with their thick new blankets of snow, bent and bowed in submissive acceptance of their new burden. The garlic at Ben's place and out at the farm slept under the mulch and the new snow. Arno and The Boys sat around Ennis's fly shop and tied new flies, told stories and lies, drank cognac and coffee. Once in a while they bought something small, just to make Ennis feel good. Three days before Christmas, Annie, feeling it was her turn to cook, had Ben out to the farm for supper. She asked Ben what he wanted, and when she finally pressed him enough he said, "I like a good Sheperd's pie once in a while."

They had a marvelous meal. It snowed those big, heavy, slow-moving snowflakes all night, and they left the porch light on so they could see the flakes floating down like tiny parachutes whenever they looked out the window. John and Ben and Annie talked for hours about the garlic crop, the plans for the next season with the house guests, and John went on for some time about how silly it was that the town selectmen were fighting over putting up a new stop sign in town. (The fight *had* been going on for almost six years.)

Ben was having one of the finest evenings of his life. He had always liked John. He loved Annie and always had, and he was talking for a change, showing a side of himself nobody but Doc had ever seen. That made Annie smile, and for the first time in a long while, she laughed hard at some of the joking between John and Ben.

Near the end of the evening John told one of his favorite jokes to Ben, one that Annie had heard a hundred times as a girl.

"Ben, my boy," John leaned forward in his chair holding his whiskey-and-ginger with both hands. "Have I evah told you about my old friend Jarvis Green over to Coburn Gore?"

Ben knew the tiny village of Coburn Gore was over on the Canadian border, but had never been there. He shook his head. He looked at Annie who was smiling as she glanced from Ben back to her father.

"Well, Jarvis had a small fahm just outside o'town and had lived they'ah all his life. One day in his latah yeahs he was sittin' on his front porch when some boys from the state came by. Jarvis asked, 'What kin I do fer ya, fellers?'

"They said they had to do some surveyin' for the state, and asked if that would be all right.

"'Have at it, boys,' and Jarvis went right on rockin in his chair.

"About four hours later it was almost dark when he went back out on the porch and saw the survey men millin' around in his dooryahd. It was as if none of them wanted to approach old Jarvis. Finally the one who spoke to him earlier came forward.

"'Mr. Green?' he said. 'Me and the boys surveyed your land, and did some parts of it three times over cause we thought maybe it was a mistake. See...the best we can figure, your house and most of your property is clear over the Canadian border! We're so sorry to tell you this, Mr. Green.'

"They were petrified, you see," said John. "You know how Mainers can be kinda stuck in their ways." Ben nodded. "They were worried old Jarvis was goin' to have a conniption, or some kind of stroke.

"But old Jarvis, he just thought for a minute and lowered himself into his rockin' chair and said, 'You know boys...that's the best news I've had all year.'

"The men were flabbergasted! 'It *is*!? Do you understand that your house is over the border?' asked the head man.

"'Yup!' replied Jarvis. 'I'm ninety-six years old, and I don't think I could take another Maine winter.'"

Ben laughed because it was funny; Annie laughed because she was happy. And it occurred to her that her dad hadn't told that joke since her mom passed away. She also was happy to hear Ben laugh aloud. Nobody's presence made her feel as good as Ben's. Not now.

As the evening wore on Ben noticed John's eyes droop and he decided it was time to head home. They were all glad for their time together and wished each other Merry Christmas before John excused himself and climbed up the stairs to his room. Annie walked to the back kitchen door with her hand gently on Ben's lower back the whole way. She was being affectionate, for sure, but Ben knew it was just as a friend, like school-yard chums. He had walked the three miles to the farm, which was normal for him, and when Ben turned to leave, Annie turned his shoulder back towards her. Ben spun around and said innocently, "Yes, Annie?"

Annie stared him straight in the eyes and said, "Ben...I just want you to know...I...I really appreciate you." She repeated, "I just want you to know." And she leant up to his face and kissed him on the cheek. But it wasn't a peck; she kissed his beautiful face next to the corner of his mouth with enough force, and long enough, that it shocked him. He had no idea what to do, so he followed his instinct and gave her a big hug. In that millisecond, he tried to convey how very much he loved her. How unconditionally he loved her.

But they split and smiled at each other and he almost walked out the door before he turned again.

"Oh!" he said, "I almost forgot!" He reached into his coat pocket and pulled out a small package wrapped in some ancient looking wrapping paper. "I brought you a Christmas gift. But you can't open it 'til Christmas morning."

"Oh, dear, I haven't gotten you anything!"

"Annie...my God, but you have." He was smiling at her, but looked sad at the same time.

Ben took a detour home that night and decided to walk through town; the snow falling down was so pleasant, and it wasn't too cold. There were Christmas wreaths on many of the houses and some of the businesses, and many of the mailboxes had ribbons wrapped around them. Ben always celebrated Christmas. But for him, it had always been a reflective religious experience, when he evaluated his relationship with God. He would prepare a remarkable meal and read sections of the Bible.

But tonight he was feeling festive. He was still riding high from the friendly kiss from Annie, and when he walked by his town cabin, he sat on the curb across the street. The cabin was finished now, except for a little interior work. The new snow on the cabin eaves seemed fake, as if it was placed there to create some sort of photo-op. As he stared at his handiwork, he wondered how much love Annie felt when he hugged her, if any. No, he knew better. His unrequited love bore down on him, as it had over the years, and a darkness began to descend into him, into that place where the human soul resides and melancholia is born. He battled back, quickly and decisively, with an efficient skill learned from a lifetime of practice. *Stay the course, Ben, know your place, lest you make a fool of yourself.*

He felt remarkably warm for the season, sitting there in the falling snow. He looked down the street and noticed somebody had stuck an empty beer bottle in the smiling mouth of the plastic reindeer in one of the front yards. Doc's office looked cold and dark in spite of all the decorations. He looked long and hard at his pretty cabin. The logs were still golden and had not yet begun to fade to gray; they almost glowed in the yellow street light. He stared at the logs for a very long time, then he knew exactly what he had to do.

He got up and limped through the quiet town towards home. As he walked through the streets, the pure white snow was stained golden by the street lamps. The rich, red neon light from the Riverdriver Café burned through the slow, thick, snowflakes making the night feel even warmer. Two carousing dogs trotted by him on their way to somewhere, not noticing Ben, as if they were late for a meeting. He liked not being noticed, even by dogs.

******

On Christmas morning Ennis Gray stayed home with his wife. Doc waited until late morning before he started wondering where Ben was. It was noon before the young man showed up, cooked eggs Benedict and got out the backgammon set. They exchanged gifts. Ben got Doc a copy of *The Endurance*, by Caroline Alexander. Doc gave Ben a first edition of *The Last Hero; Bill Tilman,* by Tim Madge. They were both very pleased. After the gifts were exchanged but before they played any board games, they each read a verse from the Bible, selections appropriate for the holiday. It was something they had done since Ben was a pre-teen.

By two o'clock, Ennis was wandering around the house, wondering what to do with himself. His wife tried to kick him out of the house to visit with his friends, but he wouldn't go. It was Christmas. Besides, the rest of the Boys would be staying home also.

John and Annie had a big farmer's breakfast. Later, as was their tradition, they had some of their neighbors over for coffee and muffins. Annie gave each household a big loaf of French bread. She frosted the loaves, and some had crushed nuts, and some had cherries and jam. She knew which neighbors liked nuts, or jam, or both. They were laid on tin-foil stretched over slabs of wood that John had worked with a plane and sanded by hand, to make something resembling serving trays.

When all the guests had left, father and daughter settled down for the afternoon. Within three minutes John was asleep in his big chair by a crackling fire, his mouth agape and snoring. Annie sat in her chair as that familiar Christmas melancholia drifted upon her. She thought a lot about Chris over the holidays, but she refused to let herself get depressed. Every time she began thinking of what she had lost and what might have been, she reminded herself what she knew to be true—that Chris would be appalled if she threw her life away. And she knew beyond any doubt that her lost love would want her to focus on the positives in her life: her father, her town, her health, his gift of fly fishing, her friendship with Ben.

Ben! I forgot his gift! She grabbed the small package from under the tree while her father snored. The sound was distracting, and she stuffed a small cushion under his head, which helped. She sat on the floor by the fire, her back leaning against the hearth and opened the wrapping. It felt like a book. It was a book. It was a small, beautiful book and it looked old-fashioned. The spine and cover were folded-bound, and there was no writing anywhere on the outside of the book. She opened the front cover and on the front end paper, along the top of the page was a remarkable pen and ink drawing of the valley, complete with the river and Roslyn in the distance. Below that, written apparently with the same pen, was an inscription;

For Annie
Love Ben

How sweet, she thought. She opened the book and there were poems, each page with its own sonnet, or verse or limerick, written by hand. They were beautiful. She started reading them, tilting the book slightly to face the fire, and tears welled-up in her eyes as she felt the anguish, the love, and desires deep in the lines. Were they Ben's? As she read more and more, she was struck by the voice from the book, and the voice spoke of *her* love, and pain. It spoke of her desires and her happiness. He wrote songs of poems, of torment and love.

She could see that the book was homemade, but was done so well she hadn't noticed at first. She held the book to her breast, leaned back against the base of the couch and stared into the crackling fire. What she read made her feel comfortable, and good, and...loved. And she smiled a pretty smile at the fire as she realized just what a gift it was.

Annie had long forgotten her father's words, "...everything gets better with time." Perhaps she never heard the words when Chris died. She was near to fainting at the time.

The rest of the winter the months marched by slowly, in northern Maine, and she talked often with Ben about the mysteries of life and death, and the acceptance and defeat of trials and tribulations. And as the snow melted in the valley and springtime threatened, some of her grief melted away also. By the time April arrived, she could go for walks where she had gone with Chris without too much pain in her heart. She even frequented The Pool up Lewis Brook, and fished instead of crying.

She began to understand the draw of fly fishing more as the spring bloomed. When her chores were done, she fished as much as she could. In March, the Phelps's sent her all of Chris's fly tying equipment, with a note saying they thought she might like to try tying. If she didn't care to, she could donate all of it to the local library or to some local youth who could use it. Chris's parents must not have realized Roslyn had no library—perhaps the school, she thought. Maybe there could be a fly tying class for the pupils.

In April, the guests began to arrive, and there were more than the previous season. Annie cooked and cleaned and cut marsh marigolds, tulips, and daffodils for the guests' rooms.

June witnessed an amazing development at the Nielson Farm: every garlic clove John, Ben and Annie planted the previous October had sprouted. They were beautiful plants, all standing in their rows, in perfect attention. There must have been a thousand of them. Annie and Ben were excited about the new crop, but John was a little worried about his ability to sell so many. Ben had explained the plan to use much of the first year's crop for seed production, and they would sell about ten to fifteen percent to cover the yield potential of the field space. But John was a simple, practical farmer, and Ben had to stop by the farm to go over it again...twice. Part of the problem was that Ben was planning to ship the garlic to foreign lands, like New Hampshire and Rhode Island. This confounded John. He was a farmer's market kind of guy. Besides, they didn't even own a computer.

In July, John, sixty-three years old, jumped down from the big John Deere (a much taller tractor than his old Ford 8N), landing his foot wrong in a furrow. He hit the ground hard and fractured his hip. Doc looked him over and drove him all the way to Bangor in his Suburban so he could have surgery. John tolerated the operation well, but it took the wind out of his sails. He would be out of farming for weeks. Doc went back to get him when he was discharged. John grumbled all the way home about the crops in the fields, and who was going to pull the corn; "Annie can't take care of the guests *and* tend to the fields by herself."

Annie doted on her father once he was home, and tried her best to keep things going smoothly. Doc and Ennis made the same walk every day so they could check in on the two, and sit with John. On one visit, Arno took Annie aside and at the kitchen table talked about her dad.

"It was a bad fracture, Annie," he said. "There's something else...it's not really bad," he insisted. "I went over your dad's overall health with the doctors down there. He'll be fine, in the long run, my dear, but he's just not a young man anymore. I'm worried the farm has become too much for him. The Boys down at Ennis's aren't doctors, and even they've thought as much *before* he took his fall. Wondered how he did it, year after year. It's a lot of work."

Annie shook her head. "I'm trying everything I can think of, Arno. Thank God for the income from the guests." Ennis came in and sat down.

Arno spoke. "You need help...permanent help, my dear." He paused for a moment before going on. "Annie, why don't you make a deal with Ben? I don't think there's anything he can't do – and just look at the garlic. We all know he has many interests, but he would ditch them all for you."

"For me!?"

"She doesn't know, Arno," said Ennis. Annie looked from one to the other questioningly.

Arno clarified: "Ben worships the ground you walk on...always has."

"*Me*?" She was genuinely surprised. "He's never said a word to me!"

"Of course, he wouldn't," said Doc. "He's never come right out and told me either. We usually only talk about wine, horticulture, history or fishing; but occasionally he would go on strangely long about you.

Oblivious as I am about matters of the heart, it took me a while to perceive his adoration of you. I asked him about it when you and Chris started seeing each other, wondering if he was all right. He only got embarrassed and asked not to talk about it. Then, after collecting his thoughts, summed it up for me when he looked me in the eye and said 'I just want her to be happy.' He had no thought for himself...or it seemed so."

Ennis, ever the quiet one, reached across the table and held her hand. "Ben could help you out, Annie; he won't trouble you with his love. But he values your friendship above all else."

Annie sat silent, but with a happiness that surprised her. She had never suspected Ben's unspoken love, but now she felt a flash of affection for that shy, quiet, listening man. In fact, over the last year Ben had been elevated in her eyes from a slightly "crippled" boy from her youth to an accomplished renaissance man; perhaps she wasn't worthy of *his* love. *Crippled*, she thought, how silly she was to have ever looked at him that way. She had felt pity, as youngsters, which eventually gave way to respect and admiration, and lately, almost awe whenever she considered his talents. The more she thought about Ben, a grateful affection joined the respect. She trusted Arno and Ellis as much as anyone in her life. If they believed it to be true, she would also.

After she'd served an early supper to her guests – a young couple from Connecticut who had showed a deep interest in the farm – she found her father in the living room, his aluminum walker next to his chair. As the young couple walked along the fields hand in hand, Annie spoke to her dad. She told him of the idea. Ben would work the farm with them, and maybe the three of them could come to some kind of arrangement. She didn't speak to him of Ben's love.

"He's a busy, busy guy," he said. "I don't think he'll have the time."

"I think he'll make the time...it wouldn't hurt to ask. I'll ask him tomorrow."

She walked into town in the morning to see if she could find Ben. Along the way she took a shortcut by walking downstream along Lewis Brook. It was a warm morning, and there was a light Hendrickson hatch coming off. It was a sporadic, slow hatch with a light but steady flight of mayflies moving deliberately upstream. It was enough to set the trout rising. At almost every bend pool and deep run, there was a trout sipping the surface. She resolved to come back that evening with her fly rod.

When she arrived at the town cabin, she could see him inside through the window, and she lost all the nerve she had summoned on the walk into town. She could clearly see his handsome head leaning over a desk of sorts, sanding the top with slow, deliberate strokes. As he worked, she watched him with a new interest and affection. Her trepidation was instantaneous when she saw him, and it lasted for days.

At one point she had a panic attack, and thought *Wait, did Arno and Ennis really know what they were talking about? Or were they mistaken...or exaggerating?* But now Annie seemed to look at Ben differently, even if the old friends were mistaken about his affections. Now she missed seeing him, and when she knew she was going to see him, her heart jumped a little. She began to explore her feelings. She wanted to be brave...she wanted to be sure...she wanted to be true to herself. So she compared her feelings from those she felt with Chris. It felt terrible to do that, but it was her only experience to draw from.

She thought long and hard about that. With Chris, she was definitely falling in love when he died, but she didn't remember feeling such a passionate excitement at the mere sight of him. She was happy last summer, and excited of course, but with Ben her excitement was…comfortable. Plus – and she realized this only upon thinking about it – she had spent much more quality time with Ben than she ever had with Chris. She loved Chris, and missed him, but now her dreams were blending together. Her pain was changing as if it was a kind of enlightenment, a *spiritual* enlightenment.

Days earlier, as she watched him through the cabin window, the warm yellow glow from a propane lamp shining on his serene, beautiful face, she knew what she wanted. She knew what she needed. Ben began carving something into whatever he had been sanding. Annie walked away from the window, her steps lighter, her heart lighter and her mind reeling with possibilities.

Now, almost a week later, she walked back into town along the same route, and stopped to wet a line in the West Branch. The first pool she came to in the river was just downstream from where the southern Twin Brook flows in from the east. The Hendricksons weren't hatching, but there were a few scattered caddis flies fluttering around, looking utterly lost. She tied on one of the little size 18 Elk-Hair Caddises Ben had given her, and caught three nice fat brookies, all about ten inches long. They were dark and pretty. Then she went about her chores.

When she arrived at Doc Warren's house, she leaned the fly rod against the white picket fence and slung her light blue fly vest over the top of the fence. She approached the front door and rang the bell tentatively, as if it might give her a shock. Arno came to the door, and though he was likely relaxing at home alone, he was perfectly dressed, as usual. He wore a teal colored stone-washed shirt tucked into some neatly pressed outdoors pants, the kind made for hiking, and some old L.L. Bean low-cut shoes. He looked so distinguished with his full head of white hair, and he so fit for his age.

"Annie!" he exclaimed. He spread both arms out and gave her a hug. "What a pleasure!"

"I just wondered...if just for a minute...we could talk."

"Absolutely, dear, come on in. Would you like a drink of anything?" Annie shook her head. "Well, let's go into the study," he said. He waited for Annie to sit, and then plunked down into a well-worn reading chair. It was a big chair, like the ones in the parlor at home, but this one was made of leather. Doc never made much money living and practicing in Roslyn, but he made more than enough to cover his malpractice insurance and to live comfortably, especially as a bachelor. Like his big leather chair, the rest of his house (as well as his life) was comfortable and suitable.

"It's a pleasure having you here, my dear. What would you like to talk about?"

"When you mentioned Ben the other day...do you really think he...*loves* me?"

Arno paused to light his pipe. "Annie, Benny has loved you all his life." He leaned back into his chair and looked straight into her eyes. "And I can guarantee it. I know you and he have gotten closer. Do I really need to know why you're asking?"

"Well, you're going to think I'm mad, but I'm thinking of asking him to marry me."

Doc was stunned. He just sat for a moment and stared at Annie, blinking, and then finally spoke.

"Oh, my Lord…you're serious." He leaned forward now and engaged her solemnly. "This is going to be difficult for you to hear, and even harder for me to say. But if we're going to discuss this, we should do it earnestly." She nodded agreement.

"You are one of the most beautiful women ever to come out of this valley…maybe *the* most beautiful." She bristled and started to interject, but Doc stopped her with both hands. "Let me finish, Annie. It needs to be said. There's no doubt that Ben's a handsome man – although I'm not much of a judge about that – but you need to be sure *you're* okay with his…physical problems." Annie cocked her lovely head and tried to speak again. "Not quite done!" And they both laughed a tiny bit and then Doc sternly said, "You must know that you could have any man you desire, dear girl." Doc finished, "That being said, I've traveled a lot, and have been to school, and although that doesn't automatically make me wise, I can say that Ben Garrison is the most fine, well-rounded man I know. He and Ennis are my two best friends. I can tell you that *I* am the beneficiary of our friendship, not them. Your turn!"

"What does a limp matter, if I think he's a wonderful person? And Arno, I do. And it fills me up to know that he loves me. *And*, it's become clear to me that he, for all these years, has always put my happiness first. That's true love, isn't it? Think of it…he would never have to prove his love for me…it's self-evident. Just think of what a husband he'd be!"

"We should touch on one other thing, dear. You do seem to be over Chris."

Annie shook her head slowly, no. "Not *over* Chris…but I've made friends with his passing. I can tell you, Arno, my old friend, it was Ben who helped me through it."

"Yes," said Doc, "he has that gift."

"That's what I'm saying…think of that. Knowing now how he feels about me, he has helped me at every opportunity through the worst of times with absolutely no consideration of his own feelings, or with any personal agenda. Just pure, selfless giving…how rare is that!?" She had tears in her eyes now, but they were not tears of sadness. They were tears from her recognition of the depth of Ben, and what a gift he was in her life.

Doc was showing some emotion now. "I have to ask…how will this come about? I don't believe he will ever offer his crippled body to anyone, least of all you…his dream."

Annie sat back in her chair, thinking.

"Annie, dear…you know…*you* will have to do the asking."

She looked him square in the face, stood up to leave and Doc stood up also.

"I have no problem with that," she said with a mischievous smile.

Doc laughed, gave her a hug, and said, "I believe that." Then he put a mock sad look on his face and said as she opened the door, letting herself out, "It's troubling for me, though…who am I going to talk to on long winter nights about Franklin, Shackleton and Burton?" She was out the door now and was picking up her fly rod and vest when she turned to him and said, "Ben...of course."

Annie stood and looked at Arno as if she was pondering her next move in a game of chess when she asked, "Does Ennis's wife still make pottery in her home?"

"Yes, she does," he replied. "She has to have something to do when he's carousing with me. What's that got to do with any of this?"

She sighed as she looked at him lovingly. "Thank you, my dear friend...you are the perfect doctor."

"Wouldn't it be great if that were true," he said, and waved goodnight.

SIXTEEN

Annie made up her mind and moved quickly. She called on Ben, and in a playful way invited herself for supper. Two days later Ben prepared a wonderful meal, as usual, with good wine and great conversation. It was too warm for a fire in the stone fireplace, but the couple ate their meal out in the greenhouse where he had placed the little outdoor table. It smelled wonderful in there, like the earth itself, and the smell complemented the wine.

She was much more flirtatious now, and when she told him she wanted to discuss something serious, Ben's attention was undivided. She drew her knees up beside her and tried to get comfortable and Ben poured some more wine in both glasses.

"Well...I don't know how to begin." She lightly bit one side of her lower lip.

"Take your time. (He took a sip.)We have nowhere to go."

"That's partly it." (She was adlibbing now...it's not what she wanted to say.)

"*What's* partly it?"

She adjusted how she sat in the chair, and faced him with perfect posture.

"This past year we've become closer. I think you know that." Ben nodded and smiled. "But I'm trying to tell you that for me, I've become *so* fond of you. Actually...more than fond, I would say. You were right here, under my nose all these years. I want us to be together, more and more, if you're interested. What I'm saying is, I would like there to be a time...when I don't have to go...from here." Her eyes panned the cabin interior.

Ben stared at her incredulously. He had no idea what to say. He was, at the very least, overwhelmed. His mind raced. He fought hard for the right words to say. He knew whatever he did say would change his life forever—everything would change, for better or for worse. Was he good enough for her? Good enough as a dear friend, surely, but as a boyfriend or a partner he was uncertain. He had never been someone's boyfriend before.

Ben wanted to say something romantic, or at least profound. But as the seconds ticked away he decided instead to go on instinct. He reached out across the tiny table with his left hand and took her right hand and held it firmly. With his right hand he gently touched her left cheek so softly she hardly felt him. He could see in her eyes that she was well aware of his affections for her. Now he knew there were no words for what they were both feeling. He didn't speak at all. He leaned across the table and touched his lips to hers, and felt an explosion of emotions such as he never thought possible, as if there was a breech in a dam that had held back the water for a hundred years. They held each other, and they wept.

Their bond over the next few weeks was meteoric, or so it seemed to others, but not to them—it actually had existed for a very long time. It was just now uncased. Ben and Annie were, as a couple, a miracle of affection. They could not keep their hands off each other. Whenever they drove anywhere, Ben would stop the Bronco in the middle of nowhere just to stop and kiss her. Then he would drive on, and he would do it again.

There is a nice little restaurant in town called the Bear Flag. It was started by a man who moved to the valley from California and was a die-hard Steinbeck fan. He named the place after a building in one of the author's novels. He even had hung behind the tiny bar, an autographed photo of the author's truck camper in which he lived while writing *Travels with Charley*. Annie asked Ben to go there for a sit-down supper one Saturday night.

The Bear Flag served a smattering of fake Southern California cuisine intermingled with some Americanized Mexican food, and one Philippino dish the cook just happened to know how to make – he had learned how from a stewardess he lived with for a couple of months in his youth.

Ben had been there once before with Doc and Ennis, but he was so much better a chef that he preferred to cook at home. But that wasn't the only reason. He disliked public places where people might judge him because of his brace, or his limp, a fear that turned out to be almost entirely imagined. Annie was downright giddy for most of the evening, and when they arrived at the restaurant she led the way. She chose the table and the wine. Ben was along for the ride. It seemed as if Annie knew everyone working there. Everybody smiled a lot and Annie smiled back. When their waitress introduced herself, it seemed to Ben that she must have been one of his date's old friends, but Annie never acknowledged that.

She ordered some sort of So-Cal chicken dish, and Ben took a chance on the venison with a sherry-mushroom sauce. He was happy to be with her, but he did feel a bit uncomfortable a few times when it seemed as though his peripheral vision caught someone looking at him through the little plexiglass windows in the swinging kitchen doors. He would look over quickly and as discreetly as he could, but each time nobody was there. Perhaps they were only noticing the odd couple, Annie being the town's golden girl, and Ben being the capable hermit factotum. Or maybe there had been no face in the window at all. Either way, it was unnerving.

Once they started the meal, Annie asked for his attention (which was at every moment undeniably hers anyway), and recited a short poem she had written for him. She seemed very nervous. She ate slowly, which was unlike her (she *was* a farm girl) and she watched him intently. Twenty-five minutes into the meal, Ben cut a piece of venison and swiped some of the sauce with the meat. There was something on his plate he hadn't noticed. There were letters glazed onto the plate.

He stared puzzled at the markings, and moved more of the sauce around, first with his fork, and then with a dinner roll. He looked into the plate and put the dinner roll to the side, and stared for half a minute and it seemed like hours. His life...Annie's life, the town, the valley, the river, his friends, the farm...everything melded into one and then exploded again. Out from the abyss and into the starry sky, his world of fear and desire collided with hope and reality. There on the white plate were the light blue words baked into the glazing:

**My Dear,
I love you.
Will you marry me?**

Annie knew he saw the inscription. Ben knew what he wanted to do. The amazement in his eyes shone with unbelievable joy. But he wanted so much to pretend to cover up the words with the sauce, lean forward, and whisper to Annie, "This is embarrassing...the waitress gave me some other guy's plate!" But he couldn't do that. He held out his hands and took both of hers.

"Oh, God, Annie, I would love to marry you...I've dreamt of it many times...have for years. But you're ...you could marry someone better off than me, both financially and physically." He all but mentioned the Sprengle's and the spine problems.

She enveloped him with a warm, heartfelt smile that said, *Oh, Ben, you don't understand the depth of my love for you.* The smile made him more relaxed and comfortable in the most important hour of his entire life. But the words that came from her lips were good enough; "Honey...I love *everything* about you. You've made me happier than I've ever been. You make me feel free, and clean and...*whole*. Once I realized what kind of a man you are, I knew in a heartbeat I wanted you. There's no one on earth I'd rather face life's trials and tribulations – and wonders—with."

She held his hands tightly and lifted them up so they both rested their elbows on the table and said, "Mr. Garrison...will you marry me?"

He was taken off-guard, to say the least. His mind raced. *Was this some sort of late-blooming rebound?* No. He could see in her eyes, it was what she really wanted. He could sense her hope, and her excitement. She meant it.

He shook his head, slowly from side to side and mumbled, "This can't be happening," and then said clearly, "Of course I will, you nut case."

Annie shot around the table, and threw her arms around his neck and kissed him. It was only at that point he came back to earth and he realized they were in a public place. Stunned, he had forgotten about everyone else. The place erupted in applause. The waitress and two others burst from behind the swinging kitchen doors, followed by the cook carrying two champagne bottles. "They were all in on it," Annie whispered. Doc and Ennis and Ennis's wife came through the foyer from the little bar in the next room. Ben was no longer embarrassed. In one defining moment, Annie had beaten some of the shyness out of him. At least part of his shell was shattered. And it would turn out later it was shattered just enough.

******

They left the Bear Flag that night after many toasts, jokes and slaps on the back. There were tears of joy, and barrels of laughter. The cook wrapped the proposal plate in a box for the couple. When the party was finally over, one of the Boys tried to walk home alone, but instead of taking a left out of the door he went right and got lost. He was found the next day sleeping in an abandoned gauging house six miles upriver.

Annie and Ben took a right out the door also, because Ben said it was time he showed her something. "As it turns out," he said, "I have an engagement present for you." The two walked down the hill, into the heart of downtown, and past Arno's office and across the street to the town cabin. Once at the door, Ben stopped Annie and said, "I'm finished. I wanted you to be the first to know."

"The first to know what? That you're done building it?"

"Not exactly. The first to know *why* I built it." She looked at him with a curious grin as he opened the front door and flicked on a light switch. Annie's mouth dropped open as she surveyed the big main room. All four walls were bookcases. There were more racks on casters lined up in two rows, one to the left and one to the right of center. There were three rectangular tables with nonmatching straight-backed chairs, and in each corner were stuffed comfy chairs with little end tables with lamps on them. In the corner opposite the fieldstone fireplace was an old, restored, tiny wood stove. It was ornate and it was beautiful.

There were books everywhere on the shelves and racks. Annie was speechless as she walked around the room, taking it all in. Ben stood still, watching her with his hands clasped behind his back. There were two sets of encyclopedias. There was a section of medical books, and one section for travel. There were books next to one side of the fireplace about the Poles, North and South, and on the other side was a whole section on fly fishing. Two of the racks were filled with magazines: *National Geographic*, *Smithsonian* and assorted rags about archeology, anthropology and other science periodicals.

There was a small desk with the beginnings of a catalogue system. There was a ceiling fan in the center of the room. As she looked around she looked up at Chris's inscription in the beam. Still she said nothing...still she was awe-struck. So much work...so much dedication. Tears welled up in her eyes again. He had built not just a library for the town, but a beautiful, warm, inviting library— the first ever in

Roz, and the most beautiful she had ever seen. That's why he had saved every piece of literature he could get his hands on for those many years! After long minutes she turned to him and stepped towards him with her arms outstretched. After she held him, she kissed him and then looked at him accusatively and said, "How is this going to work if you're always making me cry?"

"Well..." He wiped her cheek with the back of his hand, and stared at her eyes. "Don't dry them just yet; there's one more thing. I've made a sign, but I wanted your consent before I hang it."

"*My* consent?"

Ben took her by the hand to the main desk and pulled a slip cover off the top. There was the sign, a six foot by three foot hand-carved thing of beauty. Annie's mouth dropped open again. It read;

CHRIS PHELPS MEMORIAL LIBRARY
Roslyn, Maine

She openly wept in his arms. "Oh Ben, I love you so much! It's amazing, but I think I always *have!*"

******

People in the valley still talk about the wedding. Every soul in Roslyn was in some way involved. Arno Warren wore his kilt, and even though they were in their sixties, Ennis still jokingly hiked up the back of his kilt at the reception – which was at the library and in the vacant lot next door – and no, the old doctor *was* wearing undergarments.

The orthopaedist from Bangor who treated Ben as a youngster drove up to attend, and then went fishing with Arno and Ennis. Arno had to ask permission from Ben and Annie, as he was the best man. But in Roz, fishing trumps weddings, parties and sometimes even funerals.

The Phelps's came, and with them news for the bride's father that during their visit the previous summer, they had met a young couple from New York who had kept in touch with them. The couple owned three health food stores in southern New England, and an organic food distributorship. They would be coming up in a month to talk to the Nielsons about their garlic. They wanted to arrange to buy all the garlic they could produce on their farm to be sold internationally.

Richard and Sandy Phelps became a treasured part of the community. They arrived in town every spring and fall. They would first visit Chris's grave, and sit on the little wooden bench at the cemetery. Then they would spend time with many of the townspeople. There was a five kilometer fun run each autumn to raise money for new acquisitions for the library, and a stipulation of the race was that each participant had to wear something embarrassing. One year Mr. Phelps wore a grass skirt somebody produced, and he was a good sport about it. There was always a big pot luck dinner at the library after the race, and each autumn, before the Phelpses left for home there would be a big, anonymous check for the library. The library, incidentally, was something Chris's parents never quite got over. It meant everything to them, and they told a great many people in their circles how beautiful it was. There was even an article about it in a New York magazine. Roslyn became their second home. John Nielson, Arno,

Ennis and his wife, Ben and Annie all became an extended family.

The farm and the guest house flourished, thanks to Ben. Eventually the only crop grown for sale was the garlic. In fact, Nielson's Garlic Farm became the largest garlic producer in the state by far, with shipping contracts as far away as Europe. People came from all over the country to fish and to stay at the farm. Over time the quality of Ben's meals became legendary. Rooms were booked three years in advance. Some of the guests were surprised to find such a beautiful woman as the hostess, and a husband with a bent back and a limp. It was clear to see that she adored her man – and their children, who were all three handsome and smart, and not one of them had the slightest hint of a limp.

In their spare time Ben and Annie maintained the library, and fished as often as they could. The children all fly fished. Annie taught her daughter in the same golden meadow along Lewis Brook where Chris had given her that first casting lesson. Often the husband and wife went alone to fish the caddis hatches in the big pools in the lower West Branch. They caught salmon, and brook trout, and studied the insects they found on the water and in the bushes amongst the boulders. Sometimes they talked about new fly patterns they would tie when the snows came. And sometimes they didn't fish, or even think of fishing. They just sat on the bank and contemplated all they had accomplished, and their love for one another and paid homage to those that helped them see the way.

Annie – and everyone else in Roslyn, for that matter – never forgot the optimistic spirit that was such a big part of Chris's personality. Ben made sure of that.

Even now, in the springtime, Annie still sneaks off alone and hikes the trail up Lewis Brook to The Pool. She fishes sometimes, or sits on the flat rock at the tail of the pool, and looks at the boulders, and the cedars, and the ferns hanging down; she watches the water, and she remembers. There's no longing—she's happier than she could ever dream. She simply tries to honor Chris's memory, and appreciate his gifts to her – one magnificent gift in particular. And occasionally when she's at The Pool, she rises up from the rock with a tear in her eye, and does in fact raise up her arms, and laughs and laughs into the sky.

ACKNOWLEDGEMENTS

The River Home is a familiar story, one told hundreds of times throughout the ages. My variation came to me in the half-sleep of a late night. Tossing and turning, my wife asked me what was wrong. I explained that I had just "experienced" an entire story, from beginning to end. I hadn't been dreaming, but I hadn't been thinking either. She made me get up and write it down. Nothing of the sort has happened to me before or since.

Typically, my writing requires much research and leg work and a lot of help along the way from a myriad of people. It is the *process* of writing a book of essays that I enjoy so much.

Since this project required no assistance during the writing, I suppose I just need to thank my wife, Lisa, for seeing the thing through.

I would also like to thank friends like Doug Oldham, Monica Coffey, and Alan Comeau for always being supportive, and to Craig Williamson – for the support *and* for throwing the best book-coming-out parties ever.

It's hard simply to say "Thank You" to siblings (not just because there are seven of them), but even at the age of fifty-four I still am re-learning the old lesson that in most people's lives there is none such a bond as family.

So thank you to my seven siblings. Thank you for continuing to mother me, for helping with the kids throughout the years, for doing my taxes. Thank you Patty for all the cookies...I can see I can't get out of this without naming you all; Thank you Ray, Sharon,

Judy, Patty, Mary, Cindy and Teri for always being there.

Thanks to Tom Merchant from *Rocks & Sticks Photography* for the great shot of the West Branch of the Penobscot River, and to Theresa from *Theresa Cucinotti Photography* for the beautiful cover shot.

Lastly, I'd like to thank Patricia Newell from North Country Press and her family. As an independent, traditional book publisher she is choosing to use her time here wisely, producing great books for people to enjoy and to learn from. In such a quickly-evolving mass-media world, she is fighting the good fight. Many thanks, Pat.

About the Author

Dee has worked as a farmer, a photographer, an orthopaedic physician's assistant, a fishing & mountaineering guide, a semi-pro wide receiver, and lots of other things that often ended up being nothing more than "experiences." In one of his journals from his twenties, one can read that he hoped to "*beat, pound, and mold all these eclectic experiences into something useful.*" Wow.

Born with a wanderlust in Bangor, Maine, once old enough, he hit the road west with a guitar, one duffle bag, a light nylon parka and (according to the journal from that year) eighty-seven dollars. For more than twenty years he was "in the right places at the right times." He found whatever devices he could to travel the world. Photography and mountaineering were the keys.

Living in Jackson, Wyoming, in the 1980's was Heaven, he recalls...he was climbing or fly fishing every second he could. Eventually, he learned that in spite of being only an average photographer, if he was willing to crawl on his belly for a mile in the mud, or not be adverse to being in harm's way to get an image, photography might take him places. It did; to places like El Salvador, Peru, the Arctic, Europe, Nicaragua, Venezuela, Iraq, Israel, Egypt, Ecuador, Jordan, the UK, Panama, and many places in between.

No matter what he was doing, or where he was going, he was always in the company of a book, a journal, and a fly rod. When he wasn't taking pictures or interviewing people, he rigged up his old

Sage fly rod and fished every ditch that might hold fish. Now he writes about those experiences.

Dee lives in Bradley, Maine, with his wife and two children, who all fish.

www.ddauphinee.com

Facebook; Denis "Dee" Dauphinee – Maine Author

Also by Denis Dauphinee, *Stoneflies & Turtleheads,* published 2012, North Country Press.

CPSIA information can be obtained
at www.ICGtesting.com
Printed in the USA
BVOW03s1831291017
498971BV00001B/6/P